Copyright © 2020 by A.J. Rivers

All rights reserved.

No part of this book may be reproduced in any form or by any electronic or mechanical means, including information storage and retrieval systems, without written permission from the author, except for the use of brief quotations in a book review.

❦ Created with Vellum

THE GIRL AND THE DEADLY END

A.J. RIVERS

PROLOGUE

TWO YEARS AGO...

He never thought he would be here again. Feathered Nest, a little town of secrets. He never thought he would see these trees bloom new and green again in the February sun. The sun was still bright. That never changed. Spring weather had melted away the icy edges of winter. There was still enough cool in the air for him to pull the collar of his jacket up over the back of his neck and appreciate the warmth from a cup of ink-black coffee on his palms after returning from walking the trails in the forest.

He never got used to the shift in weather from place to place. He could go for weeks at a time, spending only a couple of days here or there in any given climate, yet it always seemed like a shock to shift from place to place. The last time he'd been here, it had only been for a few days, and it would be the same now. Once his work was done here, the gradually thawing Virginia spring would soon disappear into the already stifling heat of Florida. He'd get only a day there, then jump to the top of the country, still buried in the snow.

But that jump would never happen. He didn't know yet that he'd never see the snow.

His heart started beating harder the further he drove down the narrow, winding road. He'd been down it so many times he could have done it without looking, but he knew this would be his last time. This was to bring closure. To end what started sixteen years before. He never meant for it to take this long. He never meant for Emma to go through all of this.

The crunch of the gravel under his tires slowed and stopped. A breath dragged into his lungs, bringing in the heat rolling off the car's engine. He looked at the cabin in front of him. There was little daylight left, but what was still there illuminated years of change on the slumbering building. It wasn't what it used to be. It never would be again.

But if he closed his eyes, it could all come back. He could see Mariya walking to the bottom of the steps. Turning to glance over her shoulder at him, her blonde hair shimmering in the sunlight. Even this far away, he could see the blue of her eyes. It had been so many years since she'd danced, but her body never forgot it. Every movement was fluid and smooth, almost like it was choreographed. In many ways it was. Everything she did was carefully planned. Precise, neat. Everything went exactly according to plan. Everything was exactly where it was supposed to be. There was too much risk involved to gamble anything.

She always thought about the risk for the others. Those who had faced enough risk and who relied on her to rescue them from it. Never once did she think of the risk to herself. It just never crossed her mind. Or, at least, she never would admit to it. She never shared it with him. Or Ian, or anyone. The danger was an illusion, and her work was too important to hold it in her mind.

But he never thought about anything but. The danger was his life. He absorbed the danger so she could live her life without fear. That was his purpose, his entire reason for being.

That time with her, so many years ago, wasn't the first time he saw the cabin, but it was supposed to be the last. She was there to say the work was done and to be seen there one more time. After that, she would return twice more, but not to the cabin. That way, no one would make the connection. Without a thread, nothing could unravel.

But their plans had been destroyed. The monster came for her first. And he didn't see it coming.

It took him sixteen years, but he found his way back.

He wanted to stay there, but he couldn't risk being seen yet. He still had to wait, but the train had arrived on schedule, so it wouldn't be long. Backing down the drive, he paid close attention to his surroundings. He wasn't fully out of the woods when he noticed movement to one side. Something was there. It moved like a flash across his periphery, but he knew better than to stop and look. All too often, a signal for help is nothing more than bait. Instead, he kept his eyes focused ahead and drove out of town.

His eyes flicked up to his rearview mirror. The car behind him was there each time. Sometimes close enough for him to see the swell of the dark blue top, sometimes falling back so far, he could only see the exhaust. He didn't feel his stomach sink until it fell out of sight. Leviathan were closing in now. They'd been hunting him for almost a year, and he knew coming here would put him in their crosshairs. But he couldn't avoid it. This is what had to be done. No matter how it ended.

There were only a few cars in the parking lot of the hotel. He swept the area cautiously, checking each one to ensure they were empty, then settled in a remote spot of his own. He sat in the parking spot through three breaths, then went inside. The woman at the desk smiled at him brightly, but he didn't return the greeting.

"Can I help you?"

"I'd like a room," he said.

"Just you?"

He breathed in the question and held the words in his chest until they burned.

"Yes."

"How long will you be staying with me?"

"I'm not sure."

"Not a problem. You just let me know." She reached into a drawer in front of her and pulled out a card that she slid across the counter toward him. "If you could fill this out for me, I'll get your key for you."

He stared at the registration card, the tip of his pen hovering just above the line for his name.

Ron Murdock.

The line for his address stopped him. He could have left it blank. But the dark blue car hovered in the back of his mind, with the images of movement just outside of his vision and the sense of eyes crawling along his back. They were getting closer. But that wouldn't stop him. He had only one focus now.

Emma.

He wrote down an address that wouldn't lead her to his home, but to hers. One she might not remember, but that was crucial for her to understand. She needed to know who she really was and where she came from. She deserved to know what happened to her mother.

Sixteen years. That's how long Emma had wondered. Those questions shaped her life. They would continue to twist it, destroying who she was and could be, until she had the answers. He wanted her to know who her mother was and what really happened that night and the days after. He needed her to know why her life had changed.

If she was anything like Mariya or Ian, she would find what he left for her, even if she never heard his voice.

He accepted the keycard and made his way to the elevator. It stopped on the top floor, and he walked out into a dark hallway. Beside him, the sound of the elevator grinding back down to the floor below started the clock. Time ticked by, second by second, as he looked for the emergency exit. Dark carpeting barely dampened the sound of his boots as he ran to the end of the hallway and slipped through the door to the staircase. Swinging himself over the metal railing, he dropped down on the flight below, so he could exit onto the floor and hit the elevator button. Metal doors closed in front of him as the time ticked lower. He counted his breaths.

The woman at the desk watched him walk through the lobby and out through the doors into the parking lot. He was steady and calm.

She wouldn't see anyone else. The steps led to the back of the hotel, to the emergency exit.

He got into his car and headed for the woods. Heartbeats throbbed the passing seconds against his temples and tightened his grip on the steering wheel. The train arrived half an hour ago. He needed to get back to the cabin.

His eyes flickered to the rearview mirror to check for the navy-blue car. It wasn't there. Not yet.

He took turns he didn't need to, ran lights like they weren't there. It made his trip longer, but it might steal him time.

The woods were dark by the time he barreled into them and cut the lights. Dropping the glove compartment open, he tore the corner of a piece of paper and took out a pen. One more clue. Just in case. She needed to know he knew who she was.

Emma Griffin.

Tossing the pen back in the glove compartment, he took his phone out of his pocket. Typing a message, he sent it and slipped the phone in with the pen. He threw the keys under the driver's seat and headed into the woods. The winter air bit at his skin as he headed for the cabin. Lights sweeping through the darkness stopped his steps.

He stuffed the paper low in his pocket and ran. A car door slammed, and footsteps crushed leaves and branches to one side. Breaths pumped out white and opaque against the night, caught briefly in the moonlight as he broke out of the trees onto a well-worn path. Another train called in the distance, orienting him.

The cabin was behind him. He went too far.

But he didn't get a chance to turn. Before he even heard the sound of the bullet leaving the gun, he felt it slicing through the air into him. Pain seared into his back, lighting his muscles on fire. He pitched forward roughly, clattering to the ground in a convulsing heap. The impact knocked the breath out of him, but he fought to drag it back. He could dimly hear the sound of footsteps approaching. But these stopped when more came from the other direction. Someone was coming, and the man hunting him wasn't expecting it.

The shooter ran, leaving him for dead, but he kept drawing in breaths. Slow and steady, not noticeable. He stayed only until the footsteps faded into the night. He stumbled to his feet, still wracked with pain, and looked into the trees in front of him, trying to see who was there. Something moved. A dark figure stepping from behind a tree to look at him. It was only for a second before it melted into the darkness. Maybe it hadn't been there at all.

He turned, counting the seconds, counting the breaths, and pushed through the trees again. The cabin was in the distance. Close enough now to see the edges silhouetted against the dark. The glow of the outside light stood out against the moonlight, showing just the front of the car in the driveway. She was there.

Everything around him was fading. His vision blurred. His steps slowed. But he talked to her. She couldn't hear him, but he needed to say the words.

"It was raining when you were born, Emma. Your parents wanted you so much. Your mother… she didn't want to call anyone. She thought she had more time before you came. Someone was waiting for her, and she wanted to go, but your father and I stopped her. If we hadn't, you would've been born on a plane. You came so fast. I heard your first cries. The midwife said it would be a few hours, but it was only minutes. You started making your own rules then, and you never stopped, just like your mother. She was more amazing than you ever knew. You are her only child, the only person on this Earth she created. But there are so many lives that exist because of her."

That brought him to the bottom of the steps. His voice was faint now, riding out on breaths he could barely bring in anymore. They were taking the air from his fingertips, from deep in his toes.

"The woman that was waiting for her only had to wait three more days. Just long enough to get your birth certificate."

He forced himself up the first step.

"She had a daughter two years later. That girl has three children now. They exist because of your mother."

He made it up the second step and gripped the wooden handrail so hard a splinter cut into his skin. But the new pain kept him awake.

"She loved you so much. She did everything to protect you. That's why she didn't tell you. To protect you. She knew it confused you, and she hated that. She was going to tell you everything when you turned eighteen."

He made it onto the third step. The words were just thoughts now.

"She was looking forward to Easter. She was taking a sabbatical. I should have been there. I was waiting where she told me. I should have been there."

His fist came out of his pocket, gripping the paper and lifted to knock. One more breath drained from his lungs. Her face was the last thing he saw. She looked so much like her mother. But her eyes. They were just like her father's.

CHAPTER ONE

NOW

"A few hours after breakfast. That's the last time I saw Martin," I say.

I'm on the couch in Greg's room, still mulling over what happened earlier today with Sam, Eric, Bellamy, and Dean. The hospital staff keeps wanting to check on me, but I'm fine. This is the first time we've been able to talk about this in hours without someone butting in.

"Start from the beginning. Did he seem agitated at all?" Sam asks.

"No. When I first saw him around breakfast time, he was perfectly calm. He was already there when I woke up and had breakfast waiting for me. I asked him some questions about Greg and how they've been keeping the floor under control. There's still a lot of questions about how the two agents who were supposed to be with Greg ended up being relieved of their duties the day my father's brother showed up here. The only thing Martin could think of is the head nurse made the call. He told me about the agents sitting with Greg, and camping out on the cots in the break room for a few hours in between shifts when they are short staffed. He was fine. He wasn't acting any differently than he had been since the first day I came here. Always helpful and friendly. I'm sure he would have stood around and answered more questions if I wanted him to, but I knew he needed to go see to other patients. He was totally calm when he walked out."

"Then you showered?" Sam asks.

"Yes. I showered and then sat down and started talking to Eric about a cold case I had him look into for me. We poured over the case for a couple of hours before Eric left, and Martin brought me a cup of coffee. But I made it too sweet and couldn't drink it all, so when Agent Jones got here, I went to get another cup of coffee and grabbed a turkey sandwich. I told Agent Jones he could go home and sat down to start eating when Dean called. He was just telling me what he found in Feathered Nest, and I started to feel really strange. I couldn't focus and was so tired I couldn't keep my eyes open. The next thing I knew, I was on a gurney. I could feel it rolling, but I couldn't see anything," I continue. "I don't know when that was or how I got out of the room. Wait… what about the camera? Has anyone checked the feed from the camera?"

"It's gone," Dean says, pointing up to the corner of the room where the camera is.

"What do you mean, gone?" I frown and turn to Eric. "I specifically told you to put it back when you checked it out."

"I did," he offers. "The camera is there, but the stream was disconnected."

"It seems Catch Me got bored with that particular game," sighs Dean.

"When?" I ask. "When did the feed stop?"

"Not sure exactly. It's just not available," Eric replies. "I'll get working on that."

"You think Martin has been Catch Me all this time?" Sam asks.

I shake my head, still thinking and trying to figure out what happened. "No. It's not him."

"What do you mean, it's not him? He obviously drugged you and stuffed you in the morgue. You think it's just a coincidence you get half-frozen right at the same time he disappears?"

"Exactly."

"That... isn't actually an answer to the question he asked," Dean points out.

"Yes, it is," Bellamy tells him. "She's thinking. You haven't been around her enough to recognize that."

I roll my eyes. "If we could focus on this right now, it would be great. We can reschedule the... spitting contest for later."

"Nice censorship," Sam mutters.

"I'm in public." I let out a sigh. "Martin isn't Catch Me. I know it."

"Why?" Sam frowns. "It all fits together."

"Yes, it does. Right up until he disappears right after I end up in the morgue drawer. That doesn't fit. But none of Martin's behavior fits in with Catch Me. He's been playing these twisted games with me, keeping me on my toes and constantly moving. What good would it do him to have me here for two days before he did anything? And what does any of this have to do with my mother? Remember, all this time, everything he's done has been about my mother. He knows what happened to her, and he's been trailing me along because he knows I want to know too. Bringing me here to see Greg and then stuffing me in the morgue and leaving me for dead while he traipses off on his own doesn't fit with everything he's done. Besides, I bet if you talked to HR, you'd find out that Martin has an exemplary attendance record," I say.

"He hasn't missed the days he'd need to drag you through his sick little circus," Dean notes.

"So, Martin isn't Catch Me. But that doesn't mean he doesn't know him and isn't helping him," Sam muses.

"Or my uncle."

Just saying the word still burns on my lips, but I force it out. It's my reality, and I have to deal with it. Pushing it to the back corners of my mind is just giving him more power. As long as I'm trying to find ways to not associate with him, I'm giving him control, and that's the last thing he deserves. "He came here. He knew I was here. Catch Me is all about the next step. Everything is a stepping-stone. The bodies, the flowers, the postcard, the link. Everything leads to the next thing. But with Martin, there's no next thing. He's just gone. No taunt to chase him. No tiny tidbit of my history to make me want to keep going. No. This isn't him. He might have brought me here, but my uncle has taken over now."

"And you still don't think they're working together?" Sam asks.

"They could be," I admit, getting up to my feet, "but if they were, we wouldn't see all this back-and-forth whiplash. It seems almost like they're working against each other. Catch Me is very precise. Very secretive. Too much of this has been left to chance for them to be the same."

I move to head out of Greg's room. Sam trades a quick look of concern with Bellamy. They think I don't see it, but I do. "Where are you going?" she asks.

I roll my eyes. "Oh my god, B, I'm fine. Look, I'm on my feet. No issues." I spread my arms up and wide to show them I can move. "Now come on. We need to find any cameras in this hospital that might have caught where Martin went when he left. We need to find every camera we can and try to piece together what happened between me getting coffee and Dean pulling me out of the deep freezer," I explain.

"There aren't any on this floor because of the security clearing, but there have to be some somewhere. Most emergency rooms have them. Exits. Maternity wards," notes Eric.

We get to the nurse's station, and Amelia, one of the nurses on duty, looks at me with teary eyes.

"I'm so sorry," she whispers. "I should have known."

"You should have known what?" I ask.

"When Martin was changing the linens, I should have known something was wrong, but I didn't question it."

She starts crying. I walk around the desk and through the gap that leads into the corral-like area where the nurses congregate and work when they aren't with patients. Crouching down beside her, I wrap my arm around her shoulders.

"Amelia, I need you to tell me what you're talking about. What about Martin changing the linens was strange? Isn't that something he regularly does?"

"Yes," she confirms, lifting her head and looking at me through a veil of tears across her almost black eyes. A lock of inky hair slips from the clip at the back of her head and slides down her cheek, making her brush it away. Almost instinctively, she reaches for a bottle of hand sanitizer and rubs it in. "But he only does empty rooms by himself. If there's still a patient in the room, we make sure their linens are changed while they are getting a bath or participating in therapy outside of the room."

"And if they can't move?" I ask. "Like Greg?"

"Then he has to have someone help. At least one other person helps maneuver the patient so the linens can be put in place. Earlier today, I was so busy. The entire nursing staff was. When I noticed him going toward Greg's room with a laundry cart, I asked if he needed my help, but he said he was fine. I had so many other things to do; I just accepted it as a blessing. It would make things so much easier for all of us. He went in, and he came out just a few minutes later. The cart had balled up linens in it like always."

"Holy shit," I gasp, looking over at Sam. "He El Chapo'ed me."

"You said you woke up on a gurney."

"It was just for a few seconds, but that's what it felt like. I was lying down on my back and could feel it rolling."

"You wouldn't be able to fit lying down in one of the laundry carts," Dean points out. "It's not long enough."

"So, Martin stuffed me in the cart, covered me with sheets, then transferred me to the gurney? How could he do that without someone noticing?"

"Where do the orderlies bring the carts of laundry?" Bellamy asks.

"Some go to the laundry facility at the bottom of the hospital, and some are shipped out for laundering."

"Did you see him again after he left Greg's room?" I ask.

"He came back up," Amelia confirms. "Just like always. Some of the patients are on different eating schedules, and he brought them their meals. Everything seemed completely fine."

"Get in touch with security," I say. "Get feeds from every security camera in the place, especially the elevators. We need to find out how Martin got me away from the room and into the morgue. It's possible he transferred me over to someone. If he came back up here like he always does, he obviously didn't take the extra time to go to the morgue."

"I can't say for sure it was the same amount of time," Amelia tells me. "I just know I saw him again, and he brought the meals."

I nod.

"That's why we need the footage. If we can trace his movements, we might be able to see something that can help us figure out what happened and find Martin. From there, we can find out why he felt the need to skip a couple of steps and put me right into the cold drawer."

CHAPTER TWO

"Most of the elevators don't have cameras," the security officer tells us, pulling up feeds from various sources throughout the building. "Technically, it's allowed by HIPAA, but a lot of medical facilities choose not to put them in elevators where patients will be for privacy purposes. That's especially important in places like this where the patients are often public figures. We don't want someone managing to steal images of a politician or activist in the hospital and releasing it to media sources. But a lot of people, even ones working here, don't realize there are cameras in certain elevators."

"Why those?" I ask.

"Some elevators are used only by staff, and those are covered by cameras for security purposes. But not everybody who works here even knows they are there. This is one of them. It's a back elevator that's usually used to access the lower portions of the hospital."

"Like the laundry area," I say.

"Exactly," he nods. "Watch."

The footage is fairly grainy, but I'm able to identify Martin pushing a large laundry cart into the elevator. He pushes the button to go down and stands next to the cart, one hand rested on the edge almost defensively. Staring at the contents of the cart, it just looks like piles of sheets, but I know I'm in there. He's managed to stuff me inside and cover me up without anyone noticing. After a few seconds, the doors open again, and he steps out. Dragging the cart out, he disappears from the frame.

"Is that it?" I ask.

"Just a second," the security guard says.

A moment later, the elevator doors open again, and the cart slides back inside, but without Martin. Just as the doors close, I notice something at the very edge of the frame. I lean towards the screen.

"Wait, can you go back a few seconds?"

He stands back, and I stare at the upper corner. I point at something white.

"What's that?" Sam asks. "Is that a gurney?"

"That's what it looks like to me," I say. "It's waiting right there just outside the elevator. Martin prepared for this. He put the stretcher outside the elevator, knowing he'd be able to bring me down in the laundry cart, then transfer me over. At any step of the way, nobody would question what he was doing. If they saw him with the cart, he was just bringing laundry down. Once I was on the stretcher and covered up, he was just making his way to the morgue. I highly doubt there are many people who will stop an orderly and request a peek at the newly deceased. The only risk of getting caught was when he was actually putting me up on the stretcher."

"But he's familiar with that area," Sam points out. "There are probably routines and schedules in place, so he knows when people will be in that area and when they won't. If he timed it just right, he could have been down there when he'd have the hallway to himself. Amelia said she was too busy to notice if he was doing anything unusual. If he acted like he was changing the linens in Greg's room just a few minutes before or after he usually does, nobody would have noticed."

"Does it show him go back up?" I ask.

The security officer nods. He scans forward by a few minutes, and the elevator doors open back up. Martin steps in with an armful of sheets that he stuffs down into the cart before pushing another button.

"He goes to the floor with the laundry room and brings the cart out. Then he gets back in and heads back up to his usual floor," he tells me.

"What about after that? How did he get out of the hospital?" I ask.

"The next time he shows up on the camera, it's about twenty minutes later. Here." He cues up another piece of film on another area of the screen, showing footage from a different camera. "This is a lobby in one of the other wings of the hospital. If you watch that door..." we follow the screen for a few seconds before seeing the door to the staircase open and Martin step out, "there. He crosses the lobby like nothing's bothering him and heads out the door. He's carrying a satchel and a coffee cup, which is no different than the vast majority of the staff you see walking out of this place. Flipping over to one of the security cameras in the parking lot, you see him get into a car. A couple seconds later, the car drives away. That's all."

"Let me see the car," I say. "Maybe I'll recognize it."

He pulls up the footage of the parking lot. The tiny figure of Martin comes out of the building and crosses into the rows of parking spots. He goes far into the back, almost out of range of the cameras, then glances around before turning to a car. He walks over to the driver's side and ducks in. A few seconds later, the car backs out of the spot and drives out of view.

"Do you recognize it?" Sam asks.

"It's a little champagne-colored nondescript four-door. There are approximately eighty billion of those on the road at any given second. I didn't see the license plate or anything that made it stand out," I tell him.

"Then why do you look like something's bothering you?"

"Because it is. There's something about the way he got in the car." I look at the security officer. "Can you show us the parking lot?"

"Emma, you should be resting," Bellamy argues.

"I don't need to rest. I just spent a few hours napping, and you know what they say... cold makes for a deeper sleep. When we got here, I said I wanted the camera left in Greg's room because I wanted it to be seen. I wanted him to come. It seems he took my invitation. You think I'm just going to let that go?" I look back at the officer. "Show me the parking lot."

The route through the hospital to the lot is twisty and convoluted. We go through two floating hallways and up and down elevators and stairwells that make me question the architectural integrity of whoever designed the place.

"Almost there," he says.

"This isn't exactly the most streamlined of hospitals, is it?" I ask.

"We actually left the main hospital. That's the oldest section. Other buildings around it were bought over the years and added onto it, but they couldn't be directly attached, which is why it ended up with all the different connection points to get from place to place. There are still some areas where you must go outside in order to access that part of it, even though the buildings are attached in some places. It can be really confusing if you don't know your way around," he confirms.

"Which Martin obviously did," I say.

"He worked here," Sam points out.

"On that specific floor. I highly doubt a hospital that needed to be pieced together from several different buildings has the same orderlies working all the wards. Not only did he park all the way on the other side of the hospital, but he managed to get through this maze without getting seen on any cameras except when he was on his way out. Why would he do that?" I ask.

"Here we are," the officer tells us, leading us out of a stairwell into the same lobby Martin had left from.

We walk out into the parking lot, and I pause, trying to orient myself. The camera caught Martin at a specific angle, and I need to find that angle to ensure I go to the right area of the parking lot.

"Eric, do you have your car here?" I ask.

"Yeah, why?" he asks.

"Because you drive a nondescript four-door. It's not champagne-colored, but I can deal with blue in this circumstance. Where did you park?"

"In the parking deck."

"Go get it and bring it here," I tell him. He hesitates, and I glance over at him. "Please." He leaves, and I look at Dean. "Can you get yours, too?"

He doesn't question me but gives a single nod and jogs off. I feel Sam's eyes on me.

"What are you up to?"

"I just need to see something. I don't think Martin was alone."

"How could you tell that? The back window of the car was too dark to see anything through it," he says.

"I know. That's why I need to see the cars. I just want to check."

It takes a few minutes for both cars to come into the lot, and I point out the two spots where I want them to park. When everyone gathers near me again, I turn to the security officer.

"Can you look at the old footage from the camera and the current footage at the same time?" I ask.

"Sure."

"Great. Will you bring Sam and Eric to the office and cue up when Martin went out into the parking lot, then the current feed?"

"No problem."

"Okay. Sam, when you get up there, call me."

"I don't want you out here without me," he says, stepping closer.

"I'm not alone," I point out. "Bellamy and Dean are both going to be here." He glares at Dean, and I reach up to turn his face toward me. "I'm alive because he found me and got me out of that morgue. Please don't forget that."

Sam sighs and kisses my cheek. "You're right. Love you."

"Love you."

CHAPTER THREE

EMMA

SEVENTEEN YEARS AGO ...

"Where is she?" she asked. "Where's Mama?"

Her father's face was the color of campfire logs long after the fire went down. It had been that way for days since that night when the dark suits filled the house, and the stretcher went by covered in the white sheet. Since the night someone sat in the living room watching TV while she cowered at the top of the stairs and waited for everything to go back to the way it was supposed to be, then disappeared before her father came home. Since the night they sat on the floor and waited.

"She's gone, darling," he told her. "I told you."

"But where is she? What happened to her?"

A gauzy dark purple dress lay across the foot of the bed. It was where she'd slept the night before, but it wasn't Emma's bed. It wasn't comfortable, and the sheets didn't smell like her mother. But Emma still wasn't even sure how she got here, or why they were here. This wasn't Vermont. That's where they were supposed to be, but they never ended up there. Her father was wearing a black suit. It wasn't the same type of suit he wore when he worked. His usual white shirt beneath it was black as well.

"Get dressed, Emma. We're going to be late," he told her.

"Where is she?" she repeated.

"You'll see her at the memorial service. That's where she is," he told her.

But she wasn't. Not really. She knew what a memorial service was supposed to look like. Two years ago, her mother and father had brought her to one. They weren't there for long. She didn't really know who it was for, but she could remember what it looked like. This wasn't it.

She shouldn't be here. She should be sitting in the middle of the living room floor, surrounded by jellybeans, spilled like little jewels out of the plastic eggs she found. She and her mother should be choosing flavors and pairing them together to make new ones.

Instead, she was struggling against the dress that cut too close to her neck and itched against her legs. Her father led her by the hand into the room. It wasn't like the one from the last memorial service. That was a big room, almost like a hotel, in a building that smelled like flowers. Not the pretty flowers on restaurant tables that Dad brought to Mama on her birthday. These were dense, choking flowers that made her throat feel thick and uncomfortable. When her father brought her to this place, it just looked like a house. There was no one else around. She felt strange walking through the door like they should have stopped when they got onto the porch and knocked before they went in.

Her stomach felt empty. She reached in the pocket of her jacket and felt the jellybeans on her fingertips. Cherry and chocolate pudding. Coconut and pineapple. Root beer and vanilla for a float.

Emma wanted her daddy to call out when they stepped inside. If he did, she would know where they were. Even if she didn't recognize it, a name would give her something to hold onto. But he didn't. He was quiet when he shut the door behind them and took a breath of air that smelled like lemon cleaner and cold. For a brief moment, Emma's heart fluttered.

THE GIRL AND THE DEADLY END

What if this was another secret? Her daddy said Mama was here. That she was going to be at the memorial service. Maybe she was here, and this was just another time that they had to be apart for a short time, but now they would back together. She would explain to Emma what happened and tell her why she had to go away that night. Mama would say she was sorry, and they'd go home. Or maybe they would spend some time here. Meet some of Mama's friends and finally celebrate Easter.

But she wasn't there. They walked into a room with three couches turned toward a table sitting by a big marble fireplace. The couches were empty, but the table had a vase sitting on it. It was a strange vase with no flowers. There couldn't be because it had a top.

"Where is she?" Emma asked. "You said Mama would be here."

"Emma, she is," he sighed, his voice soft.

He held her hand and brought her up to the table. Emma held onto the jellybeans, letting them roll through her fingers. Coconut against chocolate pudding now. Cherry and pineapple. Then vanilla and coconut. Root beer with cherry.

It wasn't a vase. She recognized it now. It was like the ones sitting on the mantle, the ones Mama used to talk to when she was vacuuming the living room. Emma laughed when she saw that once. Not just because Mama was wearing a bandana around her head and Dad's sweatpants, rolled over and over to keep them from falling down. She laughed because Mama was having a conversation with the vases on the mantle. She was telling them about Emma and Ian, about their trip to the caverns, and the kitten they just adopted.

Emma was little then. So little, she didn't know what the vases were. Mama said she'd told her before, but she didn't remember. So, she sat her down and took the vases with her. Mama called them urns. She let Emma touch them, and she ran her fingers over the names engraved on metal pieces in the fronts. Pieces like the one on the table. Her grandparents were in those urns. They were put in there in Russia and brought all the way here to be with them. That's why Mama talked to them. They were her Mama and Papa.

People started coming in behind them, but Emma wouldn't leave the side of the table. She should be home, wherever that was, sharing jellybeans with her mother. But the metal on the front of the urn on the table had Mama's name on it.

"That's where she is," Dad told her. "We'll have her now. Always."

"I didn't see her," she said when she sat down on one of the couches beside him. "Maybe it isn't her."

"It's her, Emma."

"But I never saw her face."

"I did. I saw her."

"Why did you let them do that to her?"

He hesitated like the words got stuck in his throat somewhere, and he had to convince them to come out.

"Emma…"

"Why would you let them put her in there? I want to see her! Why didn't you let me see her?"

"It's what she wanted. This is what she wanted. She told me a long time ago."

Emma gripped the jellybeans until they crushed and melted into her skin.

"But she was the most beautiful woman in the world."

CHAPTER FOUR

NOW

"Can you see me?"

"Yep," Sam nods.

"How do I look?"

"Lovely, as always."

"Thank you, honey. But I mean, how do I look compared to Martin. Around the same size? Same position?"

"Yes."

"Kay. Now, I'm going to walk down to the cars," I tell them. "Let me know if it looks right."

I make my way across the parking lot, replicating Martin's movement. When I get to the cars, I walk past where Dean's is parked, and then to Eric's right behind it.

"We can see you," Sam says.

"Now look at Martin. Watch him go behind the car. He pauses, right?"

"Yes," he confirms. "Like he's getting ready to put something in the car. The footage isn't very clear, and he's behind the car, so we can't see exactly what he's doing."

"That's alright. I don't need to know that. I just want to know where he's standing. Look at it and look at me. Are we standing in the same place?" I ask.

"It's really hard to tell. The cars are parked so far from the camera."

"I know. But just try to compare. Where I'm standing right now. Does it look right?" I ask.

"Maybe," Sam says. "It's a little off."

I shift to the side. "Okay. Now look."

"That's closer."

"Okay, look again." I shift back to the first position. "Here." I shift again. "Or here."

"The second one," Sam tells me.

"The second one," Eric's voice confirms from somewhere behind him.

"Great. Thanks guys. You can come back down here, now," I tell them.

I hang up and head back to where Bellamy and Dean are standing.

"What was that all about?" Bellamy asks.

"My hunch was right," I say. We wait for a few minutes for Sam and Eric to get back. I lead them into the parking lot and step behind Eric's car again, pausing behind the driver's door. "This is where I was standing the first time. And this is where I was the second."

I step to the side, positioning myself in front of the passenger door behind the driver's seat.

"He didn't get behind the wheel," Sam says.

I shake my head.

"No. He stopped behind the driver's door and probably said something to whoever was there, but the camera was too far away, and the footage is too grainy for us to actually see him speaking. Then he got in behind him. Martin isn't a particularly large man, so it was harder to see him over the two cars, but he got in the back seat. Not the front. That means he wasn't alone."

"So, we have to figure out who I was driving that car," Eric notes. "Do you think it was your uncle?"

"I don't think so," I say. "Did you notice what section of the hospital this parking lot is for?"

They all follow my point to look at the large letters above the overhang in front of the doors to the building.

"Women's Center," Dean says.

"Yep," I say. "And what do you think is included in the Women's Center?"

"The maternity ward," Sam says.

"Catch Me didn't need to leave a note to keep me following the trail. Martin was the trail."

"So, we have to follow him," Dean says.

"Call the police," I tell Sam as we rush back toward Greg's room. "Let them know what happened to me. I'll make a statement."

"You want to get them involved?" Eric asks, sounding surprised.

I pause and turn to look at him. A surge of anger, frustration, urgency, and sadness swells in my chest and threatens to crack my ribs as I stare into his face. The muscles of my jaw twitch.

"No," I admit. "I don't want them involved. I want him all to myself. But this isn't some nightmare I'm just going to wake up from. I have a monster in my closet and another one under the bed. I can't fight them both at once. As much as I want to, I can't. Technically, I was assaulted in there. Making a police report will put Martin on their radar. They can get people on the ground and handle more on a local level than we can without getting the Bureau involved."

"Why not involve the Bureau?" Eric asks.

"You seriously want me to call Creagan and get him tangled up in this? Why don't you just wrap me in the red tape and toss me out in traffic now? If I call him, it becomes his case, and I'm not doing that. Not again. This is mine, and I'm not letting them get in my way."

I start walking again, but Eric doesn't move.

"Am I in your way?"

I stop and turn back to him, taking a step closer.

"Eric, you are one of my closest friends," I say quietly, forcing the anger out of it. "You know me like no one else does. You know what all this has put me through. But I also know how much your career means to you. What I have to do might compromise that. I can't promise you everything is going to be by the book. I might not follow the rules. I might not do things the way other people would want me to do it. I'll do what needs to be done. I won't tell you your skills and access wouldn't be helpful, but I will understand if you can't do this with me."

I glance over at Bellamy. "You, too, B. You've both already done so much. I can't ask you to put yourselves in danger and risk your careers, your pensions, everything."

"No, you can't," Eric says. I draw in a breath, trying to ignore the sting on the backs of my eyes. "You would never have to."

"No. Please don't—"

"Shut up, idiot," interrupts Bellamy. "We've got you. We've been with you from the beginning, and we're not stopping now."

The breath bursts from my lungs.

"Are you sure?"

"Of course we are," she smiles. "Like you said, we've known you for far too long and seen you go through far too much to just walk away. This is about you, which means it's about us. We know the risks. They're worth it for you. You've cooperated long enough. If there is anyone in this world who can end this, it's you. And we're beside you."

"Thank you," I whisper, taking both of their hands and squeezing them.

"What's next?" Dean asks.

We start toward Greg's room again, and I try to gather the fragments of my thoughts and piece them together.

"Sam is going to contact the police and handle them, so they stay out of it as much as possible. We'll have them on the lookout for Martin. It's crucial they don't make a big deal out of it or get the media involved."

"Why?" Dean asks.

"Catch Me wants me to keep following him. He's dangling Martin as my next clue. But I have other things I need to pursue. If he finds out the police are the ones tracing him, he's going to do something else, something more extreme to get my attention back. They need to track him, but not make it public. It's not going to work forever, but for right now, Catch Me needs to think I'm still playing by his rules," I say.

"We need to talk to everybody we can find that knows Martin and find out what we can about him. He was chosen for this game for a reason; we need to find out why. We also need to know his basic details. Where he lives, his family, romantic partners, friends, hobbies, where he brings his cat to be groomed. Anything we can think of that might give us more insight into him. We need to know why Catch Me chose him and what he wants me to do."

"That's easy enough, but most of it will probably have to wait until morning. We can ask around the hospital and put in some basic searches, but it's late. You need to get some rest," Sam says.

"No," I tell him. "You know how this works. Time is already ticking. The longer I wait, the more likely it is that someone else gets turned into a clue."

"Or he decides he's done playing and ready to go straight to the end," Dean says.

I nod. Catch Me won't make me chase him forever. Eventually, he's going to either tire of the game, or we'll get to the end of it. Either way, if I don't figure it out, I lose.

"You need to go home," Sam says.

"Right before I passed out, I was talking to Dean about what he found in the hospital in Feathered Nest. I need to know."

"Emma, you need a break," Dean says.

"Exactly," Sam agrees.

"Then you're coming home with me," I tell him. "I need to know what's in those files."

CHAPTER FIVE

"Are you sure you want to do this?" Sam asks as we pull up in front of my house. "We could go to a hotel for the night."

"Why would I want to go to a hotel? This is my house," I point out.

"That you haven't been to in months. And after everything that's happened... "

"This is where I want to be," I insist. "I know all of you are afraid for me and think I should be, too, and I appreciate it. But I can't live my entire life afraid. That's what they want. At least Catch Me does."

"And your uncle?" he asks. "He's the one who's been creeping around here and your house in Sherwood. He sent you the necklace and planted the other one for you to find."

I shake my head, staring at the house. "I know. But that's the point. He's been following me around, but as far as we know, he's never done anything to try to hurt me. If he wanted to, he could have."

"How about Greg? He sure as hell hurt him."

I let out a breath.

"I know. There's something behind that. It wasn't random, and it didn't happen quickly. Greg was with him for two years. He took him for a reason, and he tossed him out for a reason. The way he did, it was just as purposeful. Greg was wrapped in plastic with pictures, just like the cold case Eric found."

"The man Doc Murray," Sam says.

"With the Murdock label in his clothes. That can't be a coincidence. It's too many things linked together. My father's brother took Greg because of his connection to me. That's obvious. But why? And why keep him for two years? And why throw him away like a piece of trash? It all means something, and I have to figure out why."

"But you're not afraid of him."

It's not a question but a statement. An acknowledgement of what I'm feeling. I'm not entirely sure if it's accurate. I don't really feel fear. It's not that I'm afraid of my uncle or what he is capable of. But I also can't deny the uncomfortable feelings rolling down my spine when I think about him. I've gone my entire life not knowing about this man. I don't understand it. When we were on the train and Sam was questioning me about my father, drawing out of me why I didn't believe he could be capable of the horrors we were witnessing, I told him the reason I knew he didn't do any of it was he had never lied to me.

Is that true anymore? One thing I've relied on since I was a child was my trust in my father. I've always believed in him and known he was honest with me. It didn't mean he would always give me all the details about where he was going or why we needed to leave, but he told me what he could. For the first time in my life, I feel like he lied to me. And it wasn't just one lie. It was systematic... continuous. Every day I didn't know I have an uncle was him lying to me. And it wasn't just him. It was my mother, my grandparents. They all kept that from me. But why?

"I can't be afraid of him. My mind can't take the fear anymore. I want to know why I never knew about him and what it is about me that fascinates him so much. Let him come. If he wants me, let him find me."

"Could it be your father?" Sam asks.

"What do you mean?"

"This is his brother. Could he be following you to try to get to your dad?"

"I don't think so. He didn't start showing up until years after my father disappeared. And he would have noticed my father hasn't been around. If he was after him, all it would have taken was a quick internet search, and he would have known. It's not exactly a secret that my father is listed as a missing person, and I highly doubt he's on some sort of righteousness quest to find out what happened to his long-lost brother. There's a reason I was never told about him, and I need to know that reason," I tell him.

Blinding headlights slice through the back window as Dean's car pulls up behind us. I reach across the car and squeeze Sam's hand.

"I'm sorry," I say.

He looks at me strangely.

"For what?"

"For everything that's already happened. And in advance for anything that might."

He leans to me and kisses me softly, then rests his forehead against mine.

"You don't have anything to apologize for. All this is more than worth having you back in my life," he says softly.

I can't help but let out a mirthless laugh and shake my head.

"No, it's not. But I really appreciate the sentiment," I tell him.

We get out of the car as Dean pulls a thick satchel out of his car and comes toward us.

"There are lights on inside," he says, nodding toward the house.

"Bellamy's been keeping an eye on it," I explain.

"I'd still feel better if you let me look around before you go in," Sam says, reaching for his gun.

I take mine out of the harness at my hip.

"We'll both look."

The motion detectors flood the empty lawn and illuminate secure windows. Sam tests the back door and examines the ground around the foundation for footprints. When he's satisfied, I unlock the door. It feels strange using the key Bellamy gave me rather than the one I carried around for so many years and is still hanging on my keychain.

"The lock looks new," Dean says as if he's reading my thoughts.

"It is," I admit. "Bellamy had it changed after someone, probably my uncle, came in when no one was here."

"When was the last time you changed the lock before that?" he asks.

I let out a breath and push the door open.

"It wasn't changed since my father disappeared." I hold up a hand as I walk into the living room. "I don't need to hear it." I turn around to face him. "I'm fully aware leaving the locks the same for that long isn't safe. It's not something I'd ever recommend anyone else do. But you don't understand."

"My mother went missing for four days when I was thirteen," he replies without hesitation. "I left the back door unlocked because her keys were on the kitchen table next to a note from her. I wouldn't have changed them, either."

The words make my heart ache.

"Where was she?" I ask.

Dean shakes his head.

"I never found out. She wouldn't tell me."

"You were just alone for four days?" I ask.

"No. A man was there when I got home from school. He told me I was safe, and he would watch over me, but I told him I didn't want him in the house. My mother's note told me to be good and that she would be back. I trusted her."

"So, you didn't call the police?" Sam asks, sounding something between angry and horrified.

"My mother didn't trust the police. One betrayed her once, and since then, she was afraid. She taught me to fear them."

"What happened with the police officer?" I ask.

"I don't know. But I do know the man who came to check on me was wearing a dog tag."

Our eyes meet, and I nod.

CHAPTER SIX

IAN

SEVENTEEN YEARS AGO ...

He couldn't do it. He'd been standing at the edge of the bed looking at the suit spread out across the pale green comforter from those two hours. His eyes stung. They were so dry from barely blinking. The corners of his mouth were cracked with tears pooling there. When he'd first took the suit out of the garment bag that morning, he'd noticed the shirt was wrinkled. He took it off the hanger and examined it. Without even thinking, he called out to her.

Her name had fallen out of his mouth so naturally. He didn't even have to think about it. It was as if the syllables were already waiting on his tongue and they just tumbled out when he parted his lips. It was habit, the closest thing to instinct. As soon as he saw the wrinkles, he called out for her, wanting her to take the shirt and iron it. Part of him even expected her to show up at the door with that smile, the one that said she knew a grown man should know how to iron his own shirt, but she would never want him to. The name echoed in his head long after his voice faded.

He could only hope Emma didn't hear him call out for Mariya.

It was getting late by the time he finally managed to put on the suit. He walked out of the bedroom and found Emma standing in the living room. Her hair hung tangled down her back, and she was wearing her pajamas.

"Come on. You need to get ready," Ian said, taking his daughter by the hand and guiding her into the bedroom where she slept the night before.

It would never be home. When this was over, he never wanted to see this place again.

"Where is she?" Emma asked, staring imploringly into his eyes. "Where's Mama?"

His breath felt like knives sliding down his throat.

"She's gone, darling. I told you."

At least, he thought he did. The time since he saw the blood was a blur. He couldn't actually remember the words he said to Emma to tell her life was never going to be the same. He must have. At some point when they were sitting on the floor dreading the sunrise or when she woke up in the house she didn't fall asleep in, he must have told her what was happening.

"But where is she? What happened to her?" Emma asked.

The question hung crystallized in the air between them. He could have reached out and taken it into his palm. Held it like a talisman. Mariya would have wanted her to know, and yet he didn't. The answer was so much more than what happened in the moments just before her mother took in her last breath. It was more than the bullets that violated their home and her body. He didn't know the rest.

Emma turned to look at the dark purple dress, and he took advantage of this silence.

"Get dressed, Emma. We're going to be late," he told her.

"Where is she?"

That was an easier question. One Ian could answer, though he didn't want to.

"You'll see her at the memorial service. That's where she is," he said, before even thinking about how the words came out.

That wasn't what he meant to say. He should have been more careful. Emma was detached. When he looked at her, it was like he was looking through a screen. Like she wasn't quite real. There had only been a few tears, and he only knew about those because he'd felt them soak through the shirt he was wearing that night. But he hadn't seen any of them. His daughter looked at him through still, cool eyes and waited. She waited for an explanation. She waited for something to change. He didn't want to confuse her any more than he knew she already was, but his grasp on his own reality was so thin. He felt like he was slipping from the edge of the Earth. He clawed into everything in him, digging down to his very bones just to stay conscious rather than letting himself slip into memories and let himself fade away.

Emma was silent as they drove. She didn't know this car. Usually, that would mean she spent the ride exploring it like a cave, finding all the little buttons and cubby holes, comparing the seal of the stitches in the leather seats to the fabric of the last one. But this time, she just sat, staring between the two front seats at the windshield. The sunlight was a lie. Just looking through the window, the bright yellow glow looked like heat. It was the kind of sunlight that should warm upturned faces and soothe muscles into a nap stretched across a picnic blanket. Instead, it poured down from the sky like ice.

The house on the hill was white, a shrunken version of a mansion, with columns on the porch and glass on either side of the door. Emma hesitated in front of the door. Not like she didn't want to go in, but like she didn't know she could. There was no one else there yet. The long driveway kept the house at a distance, making it look like they were the only ones who existed. Ian knew the door was unlocked, so he stepped inside without hesitating.

It was a strange moment walking into the foyer. He knew what to expect, and yet he didn't. It was all taken care of for him. He didn't have to make any arrangements or plans. Mariya had done it all. It was so much like her. She ironed out the wrinkles on his shirts and the details of her own funeral.

She never wanted him to worry or to have to answer impossible questions. The day they got married was the day they created their living wills, and she went a step further by putting down every final wish she could think of. She ensured that if the time came when this burden dropped into his hands, he would know how to carry it. Ian looked at them a long time ago, but he stopped before getting all the way through. He couldn't bear the thought of ever having to use them.

But that was Mariya. Precise, measured. Everything perfectly laid out in its right place.

It meant everything to him to have people who would handle it for him. He had an idea of what would be waiting for them in that room, but not enough to be able to fully envision it. At least they weren't in a funeral home. Mariya hated them. She didn't want to be a spectacle. She knew there would already be one. Somewhere there was a crowd, chairs in the grass, a canopy over a gaping hole. Here, she only wanted warmth.

Seeing the urn took his breath away. He didn't want to look at it. It was all Emma could see.

"Where is she?" Emma asked. "You said Mama would be here."

He held her hand tighter. The other was balled in the pocket of her jacket. She could take it off, but he wouldn't make her. He couldn't cry now. He couldn't let himself feel anything. This moment couldn't be about him. It had to be about Emma and easing her into awareness. He guided her up to the urn, close enough for her to touch it if she wanted to. Mariya had never been shy about the urns that held her parents. She didn't treat them like relics, afraid to breathe near them. She regularly took them down and held them, talking to each of her parents as she dusted them and adjusted their positions on the mantle. She would want Emma to feel the same way about her.

"Emma, she is," he told her gently, but firmly enough for there to be no question.

It was agony watching his daughter stare at the urn, wondering how her mother got in there. Ian never wanted her to have the pictures in her head he couldn't run away from. He saw her lying there; the blood tinting her hair. He saw her lifted and covered, knowing it would be the last time he saw her before she'd be treated as only a remnant. They didn't understand. None of them did. Not the emergency responders, not the doctors. They didn't know he was the remnant; he was the remains left behind.

Emma couldn't bear the idea of not being able to see her mother's face again. That she was in that urn, and there was nothing that could be done to change it. Ian couldn't explain it to her yet. One day she would be old enough to understand this is what Mariya wanted. He would never say it was what he wanted. What he wanted was his wife. He wanted to take hold of time as it rushed past it and drag it back by the sheer force of his will and the love he felt for her. He wanted to hold her in his arms rather than his palms.

But this was the only way he could make sense of what was happening. It was the only way he could survive it. He would never be able to put her in the ground and leave her. She needed to be home. She needed to be with them.

CHAPTER SEVEN

NOW

I know Sam suggested I get a shower in hopes that it would put me to sleep, but there's no way that's happening. There's so much adrenaline rushing through me right now; nothing can stop the rushing of my brain and the sharp, acute awareness of every part of my body. It's like I'm more awake than I ever have been before, but I know the time will come soon that exhaustion will hit me, and I won't be able to keep my eyes open. I only have one choice. I have to drain every second for all it has to offer. Time is ticking. I can't let it run out.

I stuff myself in a pair of stretchy black pants and a sweatshirt still in my dresser from before I left for Sherwood. It was hot then. I had no need for the heavier clothes and didn't pack any. I had no reason to think then that so many months later, I would have made the decision to permanently relocate to my hometown. When I left this house, it was just before my birthday. June heat had burned the tips of the grass in the yard. I was looking ahead to a vacation that had just one purpose. To stop me from having to think about my birthday or have anyone try to celebrate it.

But that trip never happened. Sam needed me. The first time in seven years I'd even seen his face, much less had anything to do with him. I would only be gone a few days. That's what I told myself as I filled a bag with clothes and headed out for the town I thought I'd never see again. My winter clothes were left behind. I figured by the time the chill rolled back in; I would be here. I'd be back home. Being here now isn't the same.

Dean's sitting on the couch in the living room when I walk in. The smell of coffee in the air is the promise he's as committed to burning every bit of midnight oil as I am. Sam lurks in the corner. His posture is tense, and his eyes keep moving to the dark window. He's waiting for something I know isn't coming. My uncle won't come here when there are two men in the house with me. Whatever it is he wants, he's only willing to come close when there's no one around.

"Show me what you found," I say, sitting on the couch beside Dean.

"The hospital was pretty much what I thought it was going to be. Old and boarded up. It looks like it had been there for a long time before they decided to upgrade to new facilities, and like a lot of hospitals, when the day came for them to close up, they pretty much just walked out. There isn't a whole lot of point in trying to transfer equipment or fixtures or anything from one hospital to another. When they are upgrading an old facility, there's little if anything they can salvage, much less would want to. Everything at the new hospital is cutting edge and brand new. So they just walk out and board it up with everything inside. That includes things they don't think are relevant anymore, like paper patient records," he says.

"Isn't that against privacy laws?" I ask. "Don't they have to protect the information in these?"

"Technically, yes. But only if the patient is living. A person's medical information belongs to them, even after death. It's not like anything else they possess. It's not a part of their estate, which is why they won't give it over to somebody who isn't a legal representative, like a power of attorney. It's also why facilities often don't care about medical records like this. They don't want to have to deal with the hassle of transferring them; they don't really have any use for them, so they just leave them behind and hope no one throws a fit about it."

"I guess their laziness is a blessing in disguise this time around," I note.

"In a way. I was able to get them because they were there… but so was he," Dean points out.

"What do you mean?" I ask.

"The only way Catch Me could get the scans of your mother's medical records in the first place was by accessing them at the hospital. We should have known they would be there because they had to be. He would have no other way of getting them."

I let out an exasperated sigh and raked my fingers through my hair.

"I can't believe I didn't think about that. Of course they were there. He knew we would go after them."

"At least he thought you might. It's like hidden treasure. He wasn't just going to hand it to you. You had to actually look for it. Fortunately for us, I did. And what I found was pretty interesting."

"I remember you telling me something about a nurse," I say. "Everything's a little fuzzy after that. But you said something about finding Alice."

Dean smiles and nods.

"I did. Your mother visited Rolling View Hospital a few times. Not for emergency reasons, but for medical care. The hospital had a women's center, similar to the one in the hospital where Greg is. Just much smaller. When she was seen there, she frequently had a nurse with a very familiar name. Alice Logan."

The name makes my heart drop to the bottom of my stomach.

"Logan?" Sam asks. My eyes snap to him, and he glares with a violent edge to his usually sparkling eyes. "As in Jake Logan?"

"That's his last name," I confirm. "But I never heard him say the name, Alice."

"You probably wouldn't," Dean tells me. "He'd have called her Mom."

He pulls a sheet of paper out of another one of the folders and shows it to me. I take it into shaking hands and stare at Jake's birth certificate. It's surreal, looking at it. This piece of paper marked a change in the universe. When Jake was born, more than a dozen timers were set. Lives both already begun and not even thought of yet had potential before that moment. But as soon as Jake was born, that potential was gone. Their end was written.

"My mother's nurse was Jake's mother?" I ask

At first, I'm not sure if the words even had any volume, but then Dean nods, and my head spins.

"He was already born," I say. "She'd already had him when she was my mother's nurse. I wonder if she already hated him."

"You feel sympathy for him," Dean observes.

"Yeah, she does," Sam mutters.

There's vitriol in his voice. He'll never understand. I can't expect him to.

"That woman destroyed him," I tell Dean. "She had an affair with her husband's best friend but passed Jake off as belonging to her husband, rather than the other man. She despised him and tormented him his whole life. Abused him, beat him, starved him. People in Feathered Nest didn't even know where he lived or that his grandmother lived in that cabin. She systematically dismantled him as a human being until all that was left was raw emotion and primal instinct, including taking his sister and deserting him with an even more abusive father. I won't ever condone what he did or say that he doesn't deserve to be punished for it. But the blood of every single one of those people is on Alice Logan's hands too."

"Well, she might have been a horrible mother, but it seems she was a good nurse. Your mother has a note in her file that she preferred Alice to any of the other nurses."

I shake my head, trying to reconcile the vile woman Jake described to me with a nurse gentle and caring enough to have earned my mother's trust.

"I still don't understand why my mother was at this hospital. Why would she go there to see a doctor?" I ask.

"There are several visits over the years, but the one on the paper flower had a specific date on it, remember?" Dean asks.

I nod. "Yes. It was the year before I was born. Right before she would have gotten pregnant with me. Near the end of August."

"That's what makes it especially interesting."

"What do you mean?" I ask.

Dean reaches into the medical record and pulls out a page. He hands it to me and runs his finger along a specific line of text.

"This wasn't exactly a routine visit. Your mother had a very specific reason for going to the doctor that day, and I can't help but think it's no accident Catch Me chose this date to lure you."

My vision blurs. My mouth opens, but nothing comes out.

"Emma?" Sam says. The anger that was in his voice when he talked about Jake is gone. "Emma?" He comes and sits beside me, wrapping an arm around me. "What is it?"

I look at him, searching his face for something that makes sense.

"She was there to get the morning after pill."

CHAPTER EIGHT

I hear my own voice say the words, but I can't wrap my head around them.

"The morning after pill?" Sam asks.

"Emergency contraceptive," Dean clarifies. "Mariya was worried she was going to get pregnant when she didn't want to, and she went to the hospital right outside of Feathered Nest to prevent it from happening."

"I know what it is," snips Sam. I shoot him a look, and he calms down.

"Yet she got pregnant with me just over a month later," I muse. "I don't understand. It doesn't make any sense. Unless…" I pause, not even wanting to give voice to the thought that goes through my head. "Was she cheating on my father?"

"I can't be absolutely sure of anything, obviously," Dean says. "I wasn't there, and there aren't specific notes in her file that explain the situation. But I did a little bit more digging after I found this. I noticed something else in her file, and it made me curious."

"What did you notice?"

"Where it asks who is responsible for payment for her treatment," he flips through the file and slides it closer to me.

I lean down to look at it.

"Spice Enya," I murmur, then look at Dean. "What is going on? What does this mean?"

"I don't know, but like I said, I did some more digging. It would stand to reason if your mother was going to the doctor this frequently, she'd be living or at least long-term visiting somewhere in the area. So, I accessed some of the databases I've used in my private investigating."

"And?" I ask.

"Her name didn't come up. She didn't own any property in the area, wasn't renting any of the property in the area, and wasn't staying in any of the hotels as far as I can tell. At least not in her name. So, I searched for your father's name. Still nothing. Then I took a cue from you."

"What do you mean?" Sam asks.

"Catch Me," Dean says. "Alice. Murdock. It's all in the name, right? So, I searched for just your mother's first name. It's fairly distinctive, so as you can imagine, there weren't any hits. But when I put it in your father's, that was a different story. Quite a few people under the name of Ian showed up in the area. One caught my attention in particular. Let me know if any of these looks familiar."

He takes out another piece of paper and hands it to me. It was a typed-up list of short-term rentals at two addresses. Each of them had the same name associated.

"Ian Nesbach," I whisper.

"Who is that?" Sam asks.

"My father. At least... I think it is. Nesbach was my grandmother's maiden name."

"I doubt there are many people with that name around," he says.

"Especially not in Feathered Nest, Virginia," Dean affirms.

"These are in Feathered Nest?" I ask, shocked.

Dean nods and pulls his tablet out of his satchel. He pulls up the Feathered Nest website, the same one I used to find Clancy the handyman what felt like a lifetime ago. From it, he enlarges a map of the area. He circles one finger around the upper portion of the map, to a section I barely ventured into during my time there.

"Right here," he says. "The houses were two streets down from each other."

"Were?" I ask.

"Yeah. They were both demolished."

"When?"

"Six months after your mother died."

A surge of heat rushes across my skin so intensely I have to stand up to get away from the fabric of the couch and the feel of Sam's body close to mine. I cross the living room, desperate for air. Everything is closing in on me, and yet I feel like I have nothing to grab hold of to anchor me.

"I don't understand," I say. "My parents were in Feathered Nest? Not just once or twice. That list has at least eight visits over a few years. And while they were there one of those times, my mother went to the hospital because she was afraid she was going to get pregnant. But apparently not afraid enough to stop me from happening just a few weeks later."

"There's one more detail," Dean says.

"What?" I ask.

"Those houses. The owner…"

I don't need him to say anything else. I know what's coming.

"Spice Enya," I say.

"Like the house in Iowa," Sam says.

"What house in Iowa?" Dean asks.

"The house my parents lived in when they were in Iowa was owned by Spice Enya. Bellamy found that out after I visited and couldn't find anything. It wasn't listed like a person but as a company. We could never find anything about a company with that name," I explain.

"What is your uncle's name?" Dean asks.

I resist the urge to growl in frustration, reminding myself he's only trying to help.

"I didn't even know I had an uncle. How would I know his name?" I ask.

"It starts with a 'J,'" Sam adds.

My pacing strides back and forth across the living room stop.

"How do you know that?" I ask.

"Remember the picture?" Sam asks. "The one Christine sent along with the Easter card from Florida? When we first looked at it, we thought it was your mother and father."

Realization hits me.

"But the inscription on the back didn't look right. It should have said M and I, but it looked like it said M and J."

"You're right. It's a start," I say. "It's something. Maybe it will help us find out who he is. But that doesn't explain this Spice Enya thing, and it doesn't get me any closer to Catch Me. He pointed me to the medical records because he wanted me to know about my mother getting the emergency contraception, but he specifically called out Alice. That's the big thing he highlighted."

"He knows your link to the Jake Logan case," Sam points out.

"Everybody knows about my involvement in that case. It's on the news. The question is, how did he know about Alice?"

I'm suddenly dizzy. I can't get my brain to focus, and I'm trembling just under the pressure of standing. Sam comes up and takes me by the shoulders, squeezing them until I look him in the face.

"You need sleep," he tells me. "After everything you went through today, you have to get some rest. All this will be waiting for you when you get up."

"I can't go to sleep," I reply.

"Yes, you can. Just for a couple of hours. Everything will seem clearer after you get some rest."

Dean starts packing everything into his satchel again.

"I'll come back in the morning," he says. He glances at the clock. "Later in the morning."

"Where are you going?" I ask.

"I'm going to grab a hotel room and catch some sleep," he says.

"You don't have to do that," Sam says, then looks at me.

"No, you don't. There's a spare bedroom. Stay here."

"Are you sure?" Dean asks.

We both nod.

"I'll feel better keeping as many of us close together as possible," I say.

"She would pile Eric and Bellamy in here, too, if she could," Sam jokes, with a little less enthusiasm than usual. He rubs his eyes.

"He's teasing me, but don't think I wouldn't roll out sleeping bags if they would come." I point to the end of the hall. "The room is down here. Bathroom across the hall. Make yourself at home."

"Thank you."

Sam and I go into my bedroom, and as soon as I see the bed, I feel like I can't even move my feet enough to get to it. The adrenaline left me faster than I thought it would, but those seconds were valuable, if even more confusing. I finally make it to the bed and slide between the sheets. My head hits the pillow. I can't even lift my hand to turn the light off before I fall asleep.

My mother appears in my dreams. It's not uncommon. I've dreamed of her many times in the years since she died. Sometimes it's as if that night never happened, and I'm living my life the way it would have been if she was still alive. But tonight, it's memories. Like home videos playing out against the backs of my eyes, my dreams let me dip back into the happiest days of my life, when I didn't know there was anything to be afraid of. When the world was still full of color and light. When the thought of a life in the FBI was so far from my mind, it wouldn't have even occurred to me.

I dream of smiles and laughter, of carefree joy. In the dream, I play with my mother through all the seasons and the places we lived in. We sled together down bumpy hills that send us tumbling off the curved red plastic and into the snow, then make angels and snow families. We browse pumpkin patches washed in golden autumn light and carve silly faces into them, surrounded by the smell of roasting seeds sprinkled in coarse, crunchy salt. We open Easter eggs and pour out our jellybean jewels to mix and share.

Summer was always my favorite. With burning summer sunlight

turning the tips of our shoulder's gold, my father and I splash in the pool and race down slides. We run across the yard and jump through the sprinkler as it waves back and forth. Overhead, clouds gather in the sky, threatening a storm. Mama calls out to us, beckoning us inside, but Dad tells her to come out to join us instead.

"We're in the sprinkler. Why come in from the rain? Come play!"

The raindrops swell in the clouds as he beckons her. They begin to fall, and I join in. She's refusing to come out, but there's a smile on her face, teasing us. Dad shoots across the yard, running for her, where she stands just outside the door still under the overhang of the patio. She tries to dive inside, but he is too fast for her. She squeals when he grabs her around the waist. I laugh as he carries her out into the spray of the sprinkler. It hits them, and the sky decides to join in, splitting open to empty all the looming raindrops in a cascade.

My mother lets out another playful scream and kicks as Dad, still holding her from behind, lifts her up and swings her through the water from the sprinkler and the rain spilling down. She cries out, slipping into her native Russian. I feel something when I hear them. In my dream, I know what the words mean, but it's just out of grasp. She laughs, shouting again, and I snap awake, gasping in a sharp, hard breath.

"What's wrong?" Sam mumbles as I scramble out of bed. "What's going on?"

"Spice Enya," I say, running for the living room and flipping on the light.

The door to the spare bedroom opens, and a bleary-eyed Dean steps into the hallway.

"What's happening?" he asks.

"I don't know. She just got out of bed and ran out here," Sam tells him.

They come into the room as I open my laptop and pull up a search.

"What are you looking at?" Dean asks.

"I remembered something. When I was little, my mother would sometimes slip into Russian when she was talking, especially if she was really excited or happy or angry. Any big emotions would blur the language lines. When we were playing, my Dad liked to pick her up and run around with her. She would always yell out this one phrase. She never tried to teach me Russian. I'm not sure why. But she would tell me what she was saying if I asked. This was one of those phrases I picked up on, but I must have shoved it deep into the back of my mind when she died because I didn't think about it until now. I had a dream about us playing and my father picking her up and holding her in the rain. This is what she was calling out. Tell me what it sounds like to you."

I click the little microphone button to have the translator pronounce the words I translated.

"*Spasi menya*," the voice says.

The men look at each other and step closer.

"Play that again," Dean says.

"*Spasi menya*."

"And this one," I say, pulling up another word.

"*Spaseniye*," the voice says, and they both draw in breaths.

"Spice Enya," Sam says. I nod. "What does it mean?"

"Save me."

CHAPTER NINE

"What?" Sam asks, his eyes wide and his voice thin.

He comes to sit beside me, and I point to the screen.

"This is what I used to hear my mother say. She was always joking and playing with my father. He would be holding her or running around with her in his arms and she would say this. '*Spasi menya, spasi menya.*' Save me. It's related to the word *spaseniye*. Rescue."

"But what does that mean? Rescue who?" Sam asks.

"Women," Dean says.

"Women?" I ask.

"Yes," he nods. "Think about it. Houses owned by this entity no one knows anything about. Nobody knows if it's a company or a person. It's right out there in the open, listed on deeds and medical records, listed as insurance providers. Spice Enya isn't an individual or a corporation. It's an organization."

"An underground group that rescues women in danger," I muse. "They have to stay as anonymous as possible to avoid being detected and revealing people they helped."

"Like my mother," Dean says. "She was in a really bad place before I was born. She didn't want to tell me, but I found a marriage license when I was looking for some papers for school when I was a kid. I didn't even know she'd been married. That's when she told me about her husband. They got married when she was really young. Too young. But he convinced her he was the only person in the world who loved her and could take care of her. Of course, the second they were married, he started treating her like trash. He beat the hell out of her all the time and controlled every second of her existence. She came from Russia, and he made sure she had no one. No friends. No job. No hobbies. Nothing to take her attention away from him. If she so much as spent ten minutes longer at the grocery store than he thought she should have, he would punish her. He kept her locked in the house with no phone. She was completely reliant on him, and he made every day of her life hell."

"Why didn't she leave?" I asked.

He looks at me, a cold, painful look in his eyes.

"She did," he says. "The first chance she got."

"But that sounds nothing like my mother. She defected from Russia, but she didn't experience anything like that. By the time she came to this country, she was already in love with my father. That's one of the biggest things that convinced her it was time to leave. He never treated her like that. They adored each other," I say.

"Emma, when my mother escaped from her ex-husband, she didn't do it by herself. Someone helped her. Someone whose name I heard on the TV when I was a teenager, and whose husband was there for me during the darkest moments of my life."

"My mother," I whisper.

Dean nods. "She wasn't rescued. She was the rescuer."

Realization widens my eyes, and I scramble to pull up the pictures Eric sent of the Doc Murray cold case in Florida.

"Look at the dog tag. 'Call Spice'. This was left behind in the cabin, and strong evidence suggests it was ripped off of Doc Murray before he was dumped in front of that construction site. Dean, you said the man who helped you during those four days when your mother was missing was wearing a dog tag. Can you bring up the picture of your graduation again?"

"Sure," he says. He goes back into the spare room and comes back a few moments later, staring at his phone. "Here it is."

He turns the screen toward us and shows me the picture again. I look closely at the image of a teenage Dean standing beside the man I know as Ron Murdock. I focus carefully on the collar of Murdock's jacket. Something stands out to me, and I point it out.

"There," I say. "If you look really closely, you can see the edge of a chain under his shirt. It's coming up just enough, but it's there. He's wearing one of these necklaces. That's at least three men wearing these tags. The only explanation I could ever come up with for why Murdock was in my memories was that he had something to do with my father. I figured he had to be my father's handler, but maybe he wasn't. Maybe he was there for my mother. It was him at the house with me the night she died. Up until now, I couldn't remember. I knew someone was there. I didn't see him fully or talk to him, but the TV was on, and I knew Dad wouldn't just leave me at home by myself without saying anything to me. It was him. Ron Murdock was there to take care of me that night."

"Then what happened to him?" Sam asks. "Why did you never meet him, and why didn't you see him again after that?"

"I did see him again," I say. "A year ago, when he died on my porch. My name wasn't written on that piece of paper because he had just found it or because somebody told him to find me. He already knew me. He came to tell me something, and he died for it."

"Whoever killed him must have known who he was," Dean muses.

"But why kill him that night? What was happening that night that made him come for me and his shooter come for him?" I asked.

"Because that was the night you came back to Feathered Nest," Dean offers.

His words hit me directly in the middle of the chest, feeling like they punched a hole in my ribs and burrowed into my very being.

"Back?" I ask. "That was the first time I was there."

"I don't think so," Dean tells me. "I wasn't sure when I first saw it, but I am now."

"Saw what?" Sam asks. "What are you talking about?"

Dean pulls my mother's medical records toward him and flips to a later page. He turns it around to face me and points his fingertip hard into the paper.

"Right there. This note was added into her record by hand. It doesn't look like the other entries. It's not about a specific appointment and doesn't have anything other pages do, like vital signs, weight, or complaints. All it says is seven-two-four, L,B,F, seven-eleven. Then, under it, A,L."

"What does that mean?" I ask.

"July twenty-third. Live birth. Female. Seven pounds, eleven ounces. Signed Alice Logan."

My lungs close, clawing the breath down out of my throat, so all I can do is shake my head.

"No," I say. "It has to mean something else. I was born in Sherwood."

"Do you have a copy of your birth certificate?" Dean asks.

I get up and head for the room that will always be my father's office. There's an old filing cabinet there, stuffed in the corner of the closet. I put copies of all the important papers he left me when he disappeared in that cabinet, with the others going into a safe deposit box. Opening the drawer, I sift through the file folders and documents until I come to my birth certificate.

"Here," I say.

He takes it, glances at it, then turns it to me.

"Homebirth," he says.

"Yes," I confirm, nodding. "I was born at my grandparents' house. It's one of the reasons I was so confused about finding out about the house in Iowa. That's where my father was born. I never knew that. I didn't realize they still spent stretches of time there when I was young. I thought they were always in Virginia. I don't have many memories from when I was really little, but some of them are from Sherwood. I know we didn't stay there consistently, and I don't have any really strong memories until I was about six or seven."

"Emma," Dean says, obviously trying to stem the flow of words. "A woman who has an unattended homebirth can go into a hospital with the baby to get it checked out and file for the birth certificate. She doesn't need to provide any proof of when or where she gave birth. All that matters is what she says."

"So, you believe my mother gave birth to me in Feathered Nest, then brought me to Sherwood to get my birth certificate?" I ask, knowing I sound completely incredulous.

"Yes," he says. "I think that's exactly what happened."

"Why would she do that?" I ask.

"The one reason a mother will do anything. To protect her child."

CHAPTER TEN

HIM

SEVENTEEN YEARS AGO ...

One thing this world can always rely on is death.
It never stops. It doesn't show mercy by slowing or taking a break, even for a day. If anything, mercy is there only when death comes faster.

But it was that truth, that reliable constant, that meant he could at least get into the building. He wouldn't be able to go into the room. Not with the others who would see his face and question it. But he couldn't stay away. The second he saw the announcement, he knew he had to find a way to be there, to be close to her one last time. Reading her obituary took what little was left of his soul and scattered it. She was gone. There was no question about that. There hadn't been since the night she died, and he stood, overlooked in the shadows, and watched them load what should have been his life into the back of the ambulance.

Yet reading the obituary made that pain more intense, more real. That night it had been just the private pain of the two people who loved Mariya most: Emma and Ian. And him, too. He shared in their pain, though they didn't know it. Keeping it close, holding it only for themselves, made it more bearable. If they were the only ones who knew, then she still existed. She still breathed in the minds and thoughts of everyone who didn't know yet, like a flame kept lit from a candle long after its source has gone out. That kept her real. That kept her alive.

But even that flame smoldered. Knowledge spread. It became official. It spread out, claiming every memory of her it touched. Those final breathing moments of her ran, pushing into the farthest recesses of people's minds, but the obituary ended that. It killed those fleeting moments. Her death was not final until the world knew. She was gone now. He could still think of her, but he could no longer pretend she would ever return.

He needed that one last chance to be close to her. He needed one more time to be in the same space as her, even if it was only her body. Seeing the announcement proved to him, no one knew what had really happened. It was reassuring, in a way. Not because it meant he was safe. He didn't care about that. It meant he could continue his mission. More importantly, he could ensure justice. Mariya deserved that. She deserved more than a court would ever give her.

He went to the funeral home long before her service was set to begin. Disappearing into the milling mourners going into other rooms, he walked into the building without being noticed. Death was one thing he could rely on. It was not just her there. There were more, who became nothing but memories on the same night she did. The place filled with people who wanted those last fleeting moments with them. They wouldn't notice him joining them.

Grief rarely produces questions. No one wants to pry into why you are paying your last respects. When a stranger appears at a wedding, everyone wants to connect the dots, to create those connections that stitch together the tapestry of a new life for the couple. At a funeral, no one wants a closer glimpse of that tapestry unraveling.

It was his intention to only linger at the back of the room where he could be hidden by the mourners and still glance out to see the door to the room where her coffin lay. But something drew him to the front. He couldn't resist the magnetic pull that brought him down

THE GIRL AND THE DEADLY END

through the rows of chairs and to the side of the casket. It was open. For the first time, he looked at the face of the man being grieved. There was nothing about him that was extraordinary. Nothing that made him stand out against anyone else. Yet the room continued to fill with tearful eyes and trembling hands. Layers of black fabric crushed against each other in tight hugs, exchanged for no other reason than they still had life in them to give them.

He was suddenly curious about the man, wondering who he was and what he meant to each of the people coming into the room. But he also wanted to know his secrets. Everyone has them. No one who is born into this world and lives beyond childhood leaves it without something buried deep inside them. What were this man's? What did he hide from these people? And how many of them were now hiding them from each other?

He stood at the edge of the casket and stared into the man's face, wondering what his eyes looked like when he was alive. How his voice sounded. It was hard to imagine either one. He almost didn't look real, like this was all in place just to make use of the room. It wasn't like the other times he'd seen bodies without souls. This wasn't new to him. But there was something strange about looking at someone prepared so carefully after death. It was ritualized; designed for the living, not for the departed. He knew the process of separating life from its vessel. He'd watched the moment when all the light of life pulls away from flesh and bone to turn to dust again. It was familiar to him. More familiar than life emerging into the world.

But he wasn't as familiar with what happened in the days following that transition. When the body was taken into the responsibility of someone who held claim to it, someone who loved what once dwelled inside. It was strange to see the careful, delicate way the body was treated. The way it was painted and powdered until it barely resembled the person, and then filled with chemicals in a desperate bid to cling for just a little longer.

It was futile. No chemicals, no metal-lined casket, no concrete vault could ever stop the ravages of time. The body is only lent to the soul. Once life separates from it, the earth has every right to reclaim it and nothing can stand in its way. It seems a cruel narcissism to go to such lengths to preen and pamper a body just for the sake of those who want to be comforted by the illusion of life rather than confronted with the reality of death.

He stayed there until the family took notice of him and started to ease in closer. He didn't want them to see his face enough to recognize it later. Especially if it wasn't him. He was walking a very fine line being there, just yards away from the people starting to trickle in to stand in the room with Mariya, to crush black clothing against each other because they couldn't hug her. One of them might see him and think they were seeing someone else. It wouldn't be unusual. An easy mistake when you share your face with another.

The temptation was strong. He wanted to be near her, to look at her the way he'd looked at the man and see how they changed her. He should have been the one they called. It should have been him to take care of her. No one else knew her like he did. No one else loved her as much.

Setting the program for the man's service on a chair set up by the door, he walked out of the room, meaning to leave the building. But his feet planned otherwise. They brought him down the corridor, past floral arrangements honoring the lost loved one of whoever walked by. Mariya's room was right there. He could see the people inside. He stopped himself from going in but walked past, trying to catch a glimpse. He walked past again, closer this time, and confirmed what he thought he saw the first time.

Her casket was closed.

Why would it be closed? Why would they cover her beautiful face?

The thought rushed through him and made him sick. Her face. That's what they destroyed. When Thomas and Levi shot without looking, they didn't see their guns aimed right at her perfect face. They mangled her, so the lid of her casket had to be down, shielding her from everyone seeing what they had done, what was left of her. He'd never get another look.

Turning to leave, he saw a podium. Names of the visitors filtering through the front door and to the various rooms filled the lines of the paper in the book opened on top. He walked up to it and let his eyes scan over them. A few familiar ones stood out against the others. He wondered who the others belonged to, wondering if he could pick them out of the crowded rooms. Picking up the pen, he flipped several pages in so it wouldn't be easily seen and signed his name. By the time anyone saw it there, it would mean nothing. But he couldn't just walk away. He wanted her to know he was there.

CHAPTER ELEVEN

NOW

"Protect me from what?" I ask. "What would covering up where I was born protect me from?"

"I don't know," Dean says. "But there has to be a reason she didn't want you to know she gave birth to you in Feathered Nest."

My phone rings, and when I don't move to answer it, Sam walks toward it.

"I just don't understand," I sigh. "I never heard either of my parents mention Feathered Nest. Ever. That's something I would definitely remember. And I know I never lived there."

"Emma," Sam says.

"I know I have some gaps in my memory from when I was younger, but don't you think it would have come back up when I was sent there? As soon as I went into the town, something should have triggered. But none of it looked even vaguely familiar," I tell him.

"Emma," Sam repeats. "I need you to pay attention to me."

I whip around to face him and see a tense expression in his eyes.

"What's wrong?" I ask.

"Greg's awake," he tells me.

My arms fall away from where they were crossed over my chest, and I take a step toward him.

"He's awake?" I ask.

Sam nods.

"We'll be right there."

I run into the bedroom to put on actual clothes, splash some water on my face and head, and throw my still-wet hair up into a ponytail. The chill of the air stings through the wet strands as we run outside into the glow of dawn. I didn't even realize what time it is. When my dream woke me, I felt like I'd been sleeping for only a few minutes, but it must have been at least a couple of hours. We're silent as we drive toward the hospital, each of us lost in our own thoughts. I wonder what the men are thinking. Of the three of us, only I actually know Greg. Sam is familiar with him, having heard about him and his disappearance even before he and I reunited. But Dean has only a cursory knowledge of him and what happened before my undercover assignment in Feathered Nest.

What he does know is the brutality shown to him. Part of me feels defensive having either of them there in the first moments Greg is awake. He doesn't know either of them, and they don't know him. It might embarrass him or make him uncomfortable. At the same time, there's value in what they observe and how they feel about anything he has to say. They are at a far greater distance from Greg and the situation than I am. That means they might be able to perceive things I don't just as I can make links they can't.

This early in the morning, most people would like to still be curled up in bed, especially in the sharp chill of February. But D.C. is already wide awake and bustling. People rush around to get to their buses, the metro, class, and work breakfast, and coffee. Politicians, lobbyists, business people, students. The sidewalks are already full, and the day is already long for many of the people on them. We fight around the traffic and finally make it to the parking deck.

"Did they tell you anything?" I ask as we get out of the car.

"No. It was actually Eric who called. The hospital called him. All they would tell him is Greg woke up."

I nod and continue inside. Eric meets us at the elevator, and we ride up together.

"They didn't say anything about his condition?" I ask.

Eric shakes his head. "No. "

We get clearance and go to his room. The curtain has been pulled around the track on the ceiling to conceal his bed, and I see movement behind it. For one strange second, I think it's Greg, that he's realized he's going to be late for breakfast and has just gotten out of the bed to leave.

Typical of him. Always keeping a perfect schedule.

"Greg?" I call out.

The curtain moves aside, but instead of Greg, it's a young nurse named Paula. She's adjusting his IV and stops to smooth his blanket. When she notices us, she smiles.

"Good morning," she says.

I step further into the room and look at Greg. He looks no different than he did yesterday.

"What's going on?" Sam asks.

Paula looks at me, then back at him.

"What do you mean?"

"I got a call that Greg woke up," Eric tells her.

"He didn't fully wake." I look toward the door and the sound of the voice. Amelia comes in, looking smaller and paler than just hours before. I can't help but notice the redness ringing her eyes. "I'm sorry if that's what it sounded like."

"What do you mean he didn't fully wake?" I ask. "You called Eric and said Greg woke up."

"Again, he didn't fully regain consciousness. But he showed some improvement. He started speaking," Amelia tells us.

"Speaking?" I ask. "What did he say?"

"Not much. I came in to check on him, and he was muttering a strange name. Lotan."

I look at each of the men in the room with me, waiting to see one of them give any indication they know what the word means. They shake their heads at me.

"Lotan? That's it? Are you sure that's what he said?" I ask.

Amelia nods. "It stuck with me because it was so strange. I've never heard a name like that before. But he just kept saying it over and over. The doctors have been lessening the medication that's keeping him under, so it's expected he will wake up fully soon. I thought that's what was happening, but he didn't come all the way out of it. He just kept saying 'Lotan' for a few minutes, then went quiet again."

"Is he alright?" I ask.

"The doctor came in and checked him out. He is getting better. It doesn't seem he stopped talking because of any type of trauma or worsened condition. His brain just isn't fully ready to wake all the way up yet. He will be soon," she says.

"Do you really believe that?" I ask.

It's the first time I've let myself ask a question like that. Up until now, I've just stayed quiet, assuming the doctors would give us any new information that might come up. But they've never mentioned his chances of recovery. It's always platitudes of him getting better or his injuries healing. Tests look good, though they won't give us full information about what those tests are. But now I want to know. I need to hear if I'm waiting for a chance that isn't going to come.

"Yes," Amelia nods. "I know he went through a lot, and he doesn't look the best he's ever looked, but he's going to wake up. He's fighting hard. Something is making him fight to come back."

"Thank you," I say. I look at Sam as she leaves the room. "We need to figure out who or what Lotan is. It must mean something. It's significant if it's the first thing he says when his mind starts to rise up to consciousness. I just don't even know where to start. I've never even heard that before."

"I have," Paula says.

I turn to her.

"You've heard that name?" I ask. "Where?"

She glances at the door as if to make sure Amelia isn't there anymore.

"Amelia can't know I'm showing you this," she whispers.

"We don't have to tell her," I assure her. "At least not yet. Where did you hear the name Lotan?"

"Do any of you have a computer with you"? she asks.

THE GIRL AND THE DEADLY END

"Would my phone work?"

"I'll try."

I hand her my phone, and she clicks a few things into the search bar. It takes her a few moments and what looks like a complicated series of commands before she pulls up a video.

"What is this?" I ask as she hands it back to me.

"I noticed Martin always messing around on his computer during breaks. He never wanted to sit with any of us, and when we asked him what he was doing, he slammed the lid closed and wouldn't let us see. It was really suspicious, and I couldn't stop thinking about it," she says.

"So, you were nosy," Dean joked.

"Yes," she admits, but looks at him with a hint of bitterness in her eyes. "He did it every day, and it was strange. I just wanted to know what was so interesting. Maybe get a little bit more insight into him."

"You didn't know him well?"

"None of us did," she tells me. "He's a nice guy, and when he did want to talk, it was always fun, but it was obvious he was hiding something from us. I just wanted to know what it was. So, I created a little bit of a disturbance during one of his breaks. Then when he went to handle it, I went into the break room, found his laptop, and copy-pasted the URL into an email to myself. When I got home, I looked it up. It turned out to be an online blog. It was password protected, but it wasn't hard to crack it. Lucky."

"Why was that easy?" I ask

"Martin has a tattoo of a clover on his arm and a horseshoe on his ankle. He talked about luck all the time. I put it in and the blog popped up. Most of the entries were videos. I watched the first one and it was so strange, I didn't watch any more of them. That's it," she tells me.

Dean, Sam, and Eric stuff up close around me so they can look at the screen with me. I press the play button, and Martin's face appears. He looks like he's in a small, dimly lit room, maybe even a closet. His eyes are wild, and he looks unkempt. The audio isn't good. It crackles and fades in and out as if the recording itself was done on a faulty microphone, but I can catch some of what he's saying.

"Today, I come to you again to document the revolution. These videos must remain secret for now, but there will come a day when they will be used to tell the greatest story of our time… All will learn of Lotan and his awesome power… educate all people to what he has done and the world he is creating… privileged to be among his chosen and will follow where he leads… the power of Lotan is unlike anything… bow to him…"

I tear my eyes from the screen and look at Sam, Eric, and Dean in turn.

"Lotan will guide the way… Lotan is everything… bow to him… Lotan shall bathe the Earth in blood and fire. See the glory of chaos."

CHAPTER TWELVE

"What did you find?" Sam asks, coming into Greg's room with coffee.

Dean comes in behind him with three covered breakfast platters from the cafeteria. He hands them out, and I thank him, opening a package of plastic silverware and sliding out the black fork.

"There are apparently a couple of fringe celebrities with the name, but nobody significant enough to even be on my radar, much less be deserving of slavish devotion. It sounds like a cult."

"So, still no idea," Sam says.

I pry the top off my plate and chew through a few bites of scrambled eggs.

"Not necessarily. Eric is back at headquarters running the name to see if anything else pops up. If there are any known criminals or investigations with that name, he'll find it." I point to the screen with a piece of potato pierced on the end of my fork. "But there's also this."

"What is it?" Dean asks.

"A website about Hebrew lore," I explain.

Sam leans around me to read the description.

"According to this, Hebrew lore refers to a seven-headed sea monster named Lotan, who fought against the god Baal but was defeated. Lotan is often considered the beginning of the concept of Leviathan, a sea monster in Hebrew tradition."

"And a whale to Christians," Dean points out.

"Like the postcard from Catch Me," I say. "The whale exhibit from the Smithsonian."

"So, Martin was ranting about his devotion to a sea monster?" Sam raises an eyebrow. "I've heard of some incredibly ridiculous cults before, but nothing like this."

I shake my head.

"I don't think it's an actual sea monster," I say. "It means something. He's talking about Lotan like a person, but he's not saying it like a name. Think about Murdock. It's not a name. It's a title, a descriptor. Lotan is a specific entity, and apparently, Martin believes whoever Lotan is has a tremendous amount of power and is going to take over the world."

"He must have missed the detail that Lotan was defeated," Sam points out.

I keep reading, hoping for further details that might help me understand.

"One thing I've learned is cult followers rarely make sense when you really dig down deep into what they say. On the surface, it can seem extremely well-thought-out and precise, but when you start peeling back the layers, the cracks appear. Martin is devoted because he was told to be devoted. He's blinded by his commitment to the power this person has over him. Something convinced him Lotan deserves his total adoration and willingness to do anything to show it," I say.

"Does anything else about it make any sense? Does it mean anything to you?" Sam asks.

I shake my head slowly.

"No. Wait."

"What is it?" Sam asks.

I read through the information again. Before I can answer him, my phone rings, and I see it's Eric calling.

"Did you get anything?" I ask as a way of greeting.

"No," he sighs. "I went through every record, cold case, and investigation database I have access to. I might have gone through a couple I don't technically have access to. Nothing with the term Lotan came up."

"Try Leviathan," I say. "Catch Me sent a postcard with the whale exhibit from the Smithsonian. It said it was good to be home. I thought that was just pointing to him being here. But what if it's more than that? I'm sure there are plenty of postcards he could have chosen from. It would seem a fairly miraculous coincidence he chose the specific one that has links to the words Leviathan and Lotan."

"I'll look into it," Eric says.

I hang up and open the screen Paula showed us again.

"Let's find out what else Martin has to tell us about Lotan," I say.

The rest of the videos are just as confusing and broken up as the first one we watched. We watch through each of them, turning the volume up as high as we can without alerting everyone on the floor to what he's screaming. Parts of what he says blank out, but they are all similar.

"More of the same," Dean says after the fifth video. "Nothing he says makes sense. He's just ranting and rambling about the same things. Lotan being all-powerful. He'll bring about a new world. Chaos and destruction."

"Bringing about a new world," Sam says like he's thinking through the words even as he says them. "Isn't that like that Society cult you infiltrated?"

"If by infiltrated you mean got kidnapped and nearly killed by, then yes. They talked about a new world coming… but it doesn't seem the same. That group was all about separating themselves from the outside world and preparing for the new world that was promised to them by God through their leader. Martin is talking about Lotan, almost like he *is* God, like he's going to be the one to create the new world. Not like it's something that already exists and is just coming." I let out a long breath. "He keeps talking about chaos and destruction, but he doesn't seem upset or scared about it. I think that's what he wants."

"Let me look at that page about Lotan again," Sam says.

I bring up the site again and look at him curiously.

"What are you looking for?"

"You saying that made me think of something I noticed." He reads through the page rapidly, then nods. "Here. In the footnotes."

"The mythology of Lotan and the Leviathan are often considered parallels to the defeat of Tiamat in Mesopotamian lore," I read.

"Who is that?" Dean asks.

"Tiamat," I read from another note. "The primordial goddess seen as a symbol of the chaos of creation."

"There's that word," Sam notes. "Chaos."

"So, whoever this is has not only gotten Hebrew mythology wrong but also mixed it with Mesopotamian mythology?" Dean asks. "They must not be too serious about it."

"I wouldn't bet on that," I say. "In fact, those inaccuracies would make me lean toward being more wary of him. We keep thinking cult when we hear Martin talking, but we have to think of it differently. We see a cult because we see the negative nature of it. But someone who believes it with all their being will see it as something else."

"As what?" he asks.

"Their religion. Whether they fully recognize that or not, the devotion, commitment, and belief turns followers into zealots. The most intense zealots truly think what they believe is absolutely right and everyone else has just been getting things wrong. They will pick and choose elements of different religions, cultures, and ideas, just so they can piece together their ideal version. Within the circles they create, those who question the teachings or actions are deemed non-believers or seen as not having enough faith. They aren't pure, aren't worthy. Those who believe and follow what they are instructed are told they are the true followers. The chosen ones. They are special and will be rewarded in some way.

"Everything becomes seen as a test, even when the leader of the group has nothing to do with it. They have to prove themselves at all times, which makes believers, and those who want to be believers, more intense. More driven down into it. The leader is allowed to stitch different pieces of things together to make something totally new because they know more than an average person.

"If you don't understand it or think it's wrong, you're blasphemous or too stupid, or corrupt, or misled to grasp the truth, and the cult casts you away. So, you dig your heels in. You become louder, more intense, more devoted. You prove to everyone around you and to yourself every day that you are the most loyal and adoring follower, so you don't face the wrath or lose the validation of the group."

"So, what you're saying is this is legit," Dean says.

I eat a few more bites of my breakfast. It's cold now, but it's something to fill the aching emptiness in my stomach.

"That depends on what you mean by legit. If you mean that what they do is right and I should condone everything about it, no. Absolutely not. Martin is ranting about chaos and destruction, and those videos have specifically talked about at least six incidents involving deaths. No. Not legit. But if you mean the loyalty and passion, and genuine belief in what they do, whatever it is that they do, then yes. I saw practically the same myself when I was captured by The Society. I think Martin is being completely honest. He really thinks those videos are going to be the history lessons of the future… which he believes will be a new world crafted out of chaos and lead fearlessly by Lotan."

"Now the question is, who the hell is Lotan?" asks Sam. "If Martin was a follower of Lotan, could Lotan have a connection to Catch Me?"

"I don't know. But I'm going to find out."

CHAPTER THIRTEEN

"Alright, thanks. Just keep those words in mind. If you hear or see anything that has to do with them, even if it doesn't seem like it means anything or has anything to do with anything, let me know. Talk to you soon."

I end the call and swipe my hand back over my forehead to smooth the loose strands of hair down again.

"That was Eric," I sigh, tossing my phone onto the couch. "He went through every possible database he could think of, and the only thing he came up with was a couple of tattoos. Nothing with either of those words and the guys the tattoos were on didn't have any criminal background or link to anyone who did."

"Then why were they in the database?" Sam asks.

"Murder victims," I explain.

"Could the tattoos have been added as part of the murder?" he muses. "A serial killer's signature?"

I shake my head and walk over to the window to stare out at the late morning. It's one of those days that looks totally white like the sky has been drained of all its color. It will probably snow soon. February in Virginia usually means the worst of winter is over. But maybe the worst is still to come.

"The medical examiner was pretty certain they weren't new and had been done at different times."

"The victims could have been kept for an extended period of time by the killer. You've seen branding before," he argues.

"I have, but it's usually fairly simple, and it's done with the intention to show ownership of the victim. These tattoos were apparently large, but it was almost impossible to tell how complex they were because of the conditions of the bodies. They weren't put on display."

"So, we still have nothing," he says.

"Not all doom and gloom," Dean announces, coming into the room. "I did some talking around and then checked up on it, and we at least have one detail we can follow."

"About Lotan?" I ask.

"No, about Martin. Turns out that car he got into wasn't his." He hands me a printout of a vehicle registration. "He drives a black pickup."

I read through the information on the registration and give a slight laugh. "Wow. Didn't peg him for the truck type."

"Yep. And not even extended cab. Just two seats," Dean continues, grabbing a handful of the grapes I bought from the cafeteria during a break and popping them in his mouth.

"Which means he couldn't get in the backseat," Sam says. "Catch Me wanted him to sit behind him?"

"Or there was someone else in the car, too," I point out.

"Catch Me is two people? That would explain the trains."

I think about the possibility for a second, but it doesn't sit right with me, and I shake my head.

"No. I don't think so. It would make sense for the two trains, but that's it. Everything else has been too precise, too streamlined. This guy is hyper-focused on me finding him and him specifically. Everything has been 'me' and 'I'. It's extremely organized. You don't usually see that when people are working together. Even if they are on the same page and telling the same plan, things go wrong, people's personalities come out, and you see disorganization and disconnects. I haven't seen any of that with Catch Me. This is very much one-on-

THE GIRL AND THE DEADLY END

one. It's him against me. If there was someone else in that car, that's a deviation."

"Returning to our earlier theory: could Catch Me be working with your uncle? That would explain the second person," points out Sam.

"It's possible. But that doesn't line up either. My uncle clearly had ways to get in the house to drop off those necklaces. He wouldn't need to pepper clues for me to follow. I just don't know what the connection is."

"But it's something. And that's better than what we've had," Dean says.

"That's true." I let out an exasperated sigh and shake my head. "It's just driving me insane. I know I've heard of Leviathan. And not just because it's a word. It means something, and I can't remember what."

"Could have been something your father told you?" Sam asks. "A case he was working on or something the CIA was investigating?"

"Maybe," I acknowledge. "Maybe I saw something when I was reading his files, and it just stuck in my mind somewhere."

I start towards the door.

"Where are you going?" Dean asks.

"To look through my father's files," I tell him. "When he left, his case files were still in his office. I didn't get rid of any of them."

I walk out of the room and go to the nurse's desk.

"If he says anything else, call me immediately," I tell Amelia.

She nods.

"I will. I'll check up on him soon."

"Thank you," I tell her.

Both men catch up to me as I go down the elevator and head for the car. My eyes shoot back and forth as I drive through the parking lot and out onto the road.

"What are you looking for?" Sam asks.

"Anything," I tell him. "Up until now, Catch Me has been really clear about his instructions. Even when he was leaving riddles, it was clear he wanted me to solve the riddle and figure out what to do next. But I don't have that this time. I know it's supposed to be about Martin. Obviously, he's helping or was told to do something, and

Catch Me had him meet him out in the parking lot outside the maternity ward as a message to me. But that's where it stops. We don't know where Martin went or what he's doing, so how are we supposed to follow him?"

"You have to trust the police. We all gave our statements, and they are looking for him. That's all we can do right now. We have to trust that they will do their jobs and be able to trace his movements. Once they find him, we'll figure out what we're supposed to do next."

"I want to believe that," I tell him. "But I feel like I'm missing something. Like there's a link or some sort of connection I haven't noticed. He's already proven that when I don't follow along with what he's doing fast enough, or even when I do, the results get bloody. I don't want anyone else to die because I didn't play his game correctly."

"You can't do that to yourself," Dean says. "You can't make yourself responsible for everything that happens. You didn't do this. You didn't do any of it."

"If I could figure out who he is, it would stop him," I reply. "If I'd been able to find him on the train or in Feathered Nest, these things wouldn't be happening."

"You don't know that," Sam says.

"He's right," Dean agrees. "You can't predict what he's going to do. It's not your fault he's doing these things. I know it's easy to get into that place where you feel like you caused everything. But you didn't cause this, and you can't blame yourself. All that's going to do is distract you from stopping what comes next."

"You don't understand," I say.

"I do understand, Emma. In one of my earliest cases, two children had been kidnapped. The mother was working with the police, but they didn't have any leads and hadn't figured out anything. She strongly believed it was her ex-husband. They had been fighting over custody for a long time, and she believed he only wanted it so he could get child support out of her. She made a lot more money than he did, and in court, he tried to demand alimony, but the judge shut that down real fast. She was convinced he came and snatched the children to get money out of her. So, she hired me to track him down and see if I could find the children. I located him in New York. He had been on the run for almost three weeks, and the children looked exhausted like he hadn't stopped. I was trying to decide how to handle it when I found out he was planning on loading the children up into a plane and leaving the country. I called the local police department to let them know what was going on and followed them to the subway. I saw him standing right there in the middle of the crowd with the children on each hip."

"What did you do?" I ask.

"I waited. I thought it was best if I waited for the police to come and we did a controlled, managed, takedown. I figured it was so crowded down there and it was going to be a little bit before the train got there, so he wasn't going to be moving. I just kept my eye on him, following to make sure he didn't do anything to the children. I assumed when the police arrived, they would be able to recover both of them and arrest him. I stood there, not two feet away from him. He didn't know who I was, so he had no reason to run away from me. I was close enough that I could have reached out and taken the children out of his arms."

"But you didn't," I say.

"No," he says. "I didn't. I stood there, and I waited. It hurt like hell to do, but I did. I just wanted to rescue them, but I knew I'd jeopardize the whole thing if I made a move. Finally, the police arrived, and one of them made a move toward the guy. It spooked him, and he started running through the crowd. I chased after him, but before I could reach out and get the children, the train started coming into the station, and he tossed one of them down onto the tracks. She made it but lost a leg and got severely injured and traumatized. For a long time, I destroyed myself over that. I felt like it was my fault. It was enough that I almost quit."

"Why didn't you?" I ask.

"A few weeks later, I found a girl who had disappeared when an internet predator lured her out of her house. She was alive, and I got her back to her parents. Then at the hearing for the man who threw his daughter, he said he would have done it no matter what. If I had tried to grab one of them, he just would have tossed the other one. I had to realize it wasn't my fault. As much as I desperately wanted to protect those children and stop anything from happening to them, I couldn't control their father. I couldn't stop him from doing exactly what he was going to do. So, I do understand."

He looks at me with tears brimming in his eyes, but his jaw set and serious. "Emma, I want you to know, this isn't you. You might have to be the one to bring him down, but you aren't making him do what he's doing."

CHAPTER FOURTEEN

"When was the last time you looked through these?" Sam asks as I pull stacks of folders out of the filing cabinet in what I still think of as my father's office.

"Years ago," I tell him. I hand him a stack and turn around to get more. "When he first disappeared, I spent a lot of time going through them. I thought maybe if I understood what he was doing and the cases that were taking up the most of his time and energy, maybe I'd be able to figure out what happened to him. I know he didn't leave me any information about where he was going or why, but something told me I could figure it out just by digging through what he was doing in the days leading up to when he left. Of course, I never figured that out. I must have gone through these files a dozen times each, but it wasn't enough to help me trace him."

I hand off another stack of files to Dean and get a stack for myself. We go back into the living room, and they move the coffee table out of the way so we can sit on the floor and spread the files out around us. Once we're settled into place, each of us pick an arbitrary folder out of our stacks and start reading through them. It's been so long since I've read the files, but as I go through them, details start coming back to me. I remember reading about the cases, trying to piece together what they could mean and which one of them had claimed my father's attention so much he needed to leave me in order to pursue it.

The first file I go through contains nothing that points to Leviathan or Lotan. I set it aside and pick up another. Sam and Dean do the same. For the next two hours, we read through the files, separating them out into two stacks: one of cases that clearly have no link, almost overwhelmingly tall, and a much smaller stack of cases that could possibly have the slightest something to do with Catch Me or Lotan or Leviathan or whatever we're looking for. Finally, we've gone through all the files, and I look at the stacks.

"Alright. I guess now we go through the ones that might have information in them," I say.

Each of us picks up a file, and we start reading out the details to each other. Sam has one that involves a smuggler who managed to avoid any type of detection for years because they stayed in international waters.

"The boat they used was named *Sea Monster*," Sam says. "That could have something to do with it."

"It's closed," I tell them. "I actually remember the continuation of that case. They found the boat and seized it. It was destroyed three years after my father disappeared."

He lets out a sigh and tosses the file onto the other stack. Dean takes his turn.

"This one is about a serial killer who likes to play hide and seek, at least that's what he called it. He'd call in a tip about where he was going to hide a body and start a countdown. That sounds similar to the idea of Catch Me."

"Yeah, but he was only active when I was much younger. By the time Dad disappeared, he hadn't killed in almost six years. The widely accepted belief is he died. They weren't searching for him to stop him, but to solve the cases. It's possible he didn't actually die and was just in hibernation, but there isn't any reason why he would target me. Dad wasn't one of the main people on the case, and there was never a suspect or anything, so there wouldn't be a reason to come after me specifically."

"Alright. What do you have?"

I open the folder in my hands and look down at it, opening my mouth to start talking, then stop and close the file.

"Nothing. I have nothing. This case had to do with a murder on a beach." I toss the file down with a heavy sigh. "It's reaching. None of these have anything useful in them."

Sam looks at the files and tilts his head to the side like he's trying to figure something out.

"Is this all the files?" he asks.

"Yes," I say. "It's everything that was in his office when he left."

"It doesn't look like many cases," he points out. "I don't know everything about your father's career, but from what I understand, he was important in the CIA."

"Is," I correct him. "He is."

We meet eyes, and Sam stares at me for a few seconds before nodding.

"Is. He's an active, high-ranking agent. But this is all he worked on in the months before he disappeared?"

"It doesn't seem like much," I admit. "He didn't go into a lot of detail with me about what he was working on, obviously, but it seems to me he should have been working on more. This is everything that was here tough. The Agency wouldn't disclose anything else."

"So, there might be other cases," Dean points out.

I nod. "Ones he didn't bring home with him. I guess this was pretty pointless."

"It wasn't pointless. You have to look into everything until you figure out what you're supposed to follow. What about Jake Logan?"

"What about him?" Sam asks.

"His mother was Emma's mother's nurse," he points out.

"This whole time he's been pointing out things about her mother. Maybe he just wanted her to know about her mother going to the doctor there and her being born in Feathered Nest."

"No," I say, shaking my head. I take him by the hands. "Sam, I know you hate when I even think about Jake. I know it gets to you."

"Of course it does. He's a serial killer who manipulated you and tried to kill you. I'm not a fan of someone doing that to the woman I love," he says gruffly.

"He's in prison now. And he will be for the rest of his life. It wouldn't surprise me if they attempted to keep his body in a cell even after he dies."

"He would deserve it."

"The point is, Catch Me didn't just direct me to the medical records. He could have done that in any number of ways. He specifically highlighted Jake's mother. He used pages from Alice in Wonderland and references to the mad tea party to bring me to them. He wants me to know about Alice Logan specifically."

"Were you ever able to interview them?" Dean asks.

"No. They were located but didn't go to any of the trials. The second everything happened, they lawyered up and their counsel petitioned the court to exclude them from in-person testimony because they were afraid of Jake. They felt their personal safety was at risk if they had to be in the same room with him."

"And they made that fly with the judge?"

"Apparently they were able to convince him that because they weren't in Jake's life for years before the murders, their presence would not be beneficial and could even cause a further psychotic break that might endanger the integrity of the case."

"What a bunch of bullshit."

"That was my general opinion," I admit. "But the judge bought it. He allowed them to make recorded statements with basic information about his childhood. They spoke to their family life, his personality, and what might have led to the killings. Of course, they conveniently left out abandoning him with an abusive father."

"What did they say about that?" Sam asks.

The trial was so sensationalized it ended up being closed to anyone who wasn't involved, which meant Sam wasn't allowed to be in the courtroom with me during it. He never wanted to talk about it after the trial either. He said he thought I needed a break from all the stress and emotion of the trial, but I know it's just as much because of how much it bothers him to think about my undercover assignment. He hates to think about me going through that and that he wasn't there to protect me. Of course, we hadn't spoken in seven years at that point. There's no way he could have been there or known I needed help. But it still weighs heavily on him, and he doesn't like to dwell on it too much. I'm surprised he's even asking, but the urgency of what's happening now must overrule his resistance.

"Wait," Dean says. "You've seen Alice Logan's testimony? So, you already knew her name. Why didn't you think of it when the clue was left?"

"I didn't know her name is Alice. During the testimony, she was referred to as Walden Logan."

"Walden?" Sam raises an eyebrow.

"Her middle name," Dean explains. "It was her mother's maiden name."

Sam and I look at him, and Dean shrugs.

"Private investigating has taught me a lot of skills. Skimming background information is child's play. When I found out the name Alice Logan, I wanted to know more about her. I did a check on her to find out who she was. That's how I knew she's Jake's mother."

"If I was her, I would have changed my name, too. I wouldn't want to be associated with her family or known for what she did. Of course, according to her testimony, she didn't do anything wrong. She tugged the heartstrings with a long story about how horrible her husband was and how oppressive her home life was. To hear it from her, the reason no one in town knew who she was or where she lived was because of her husband, John. He didn't want her or their daughter Sally leaving the house or associating with anyone. He would fly into a rage and get incredibly violent if she put so much as a toe outside of the line, he put down for her. Of course, that line was always moving, so she didn't know when she was going to get in trouble."

"Wasn't she the one who abused Jake?" Dean asks.

"The way he told it to me, they both did. And considering I was listening to his declaration while waiting to be sent up as a burned sacrifice, I tend to believe him," I say.

"How did she justify leaving him, though?"

"She said she didn't just leave him. She didn't disappear. Her official testimony was that she couldn't take the abuse anymore. Sally was starting to withdraw, and one day she caught her husband looking at their daughter when she got out of the shower. She decided she couldn't take it anymore and told her children, both her children, they were going to leave. She'd already gotten in touch with her sister, who lives in Utah, and they were going to go live with her. To hear her tell it, Jake refused to go. He wanted to stay with his father. She knew she didn't have the time to argue with him, especially when he ran off into the woods. So she left. She did what she had to do to survive. She said she reached out to him several times to try to get him to come to be with her, but he never wanted to."

"And Jake never mentioned any of that?" Sam asks.

"No. I don't believe a word she says other than that she planned to leave. I think she hated her husband and her son. Jake was the product of an affair, and it caused all kinds of problems. She favored her daughter, so she figured the only way she was going to have the life she wanted was to leave. I don't think she tried to get in touch with him or ever even thought about him again. She went so far as to change her name so he couldn't find her. She wasn't too creative about it, granted, but she did it," I say.

"And life after she left? Any idea what she's been doing?"

"Just living a normal life, apparently. She and Sally separated themselves from everybody in Feathered Nest and faded into obscurity, essentially. They were able to produce information that shows they lived a normal life… rented a house in the suburbs after living with her sister for a while, got a job in an office. Nothing extraordinary."

"An office job?" Dean asks. "I wonder why she would go from being a nurse to working in an office?"

"She realized she didn't actually like taking care of people?" I suggest. "Or she just really wanted a totally different life."

I reach for my phone.

"Who are you calling?" Sam asks.

"Eric. I want to see if he can track down what is quite possibly the most common car on the face of the planet."

CHAPTER FIFTEEN

"No surprise, there are far too many cars of that exact color, make, and model in the area to even try to narrow it down right now. We didn't see the license plate number, and while there are other ways that we could track movements of the cars, it would take forever, and we just don't have time for that right this second. But, I did ask Eric to pull up the surveillance at a couple of places. He sent me the videos," I tell them, opening my laptop and cueing up the first of the videos Eric sent.

"What's this?" Dean asks, Looking over my shoulder at the screen.

"This is one of the surveillance cameras outside the bus station in Richmond that was bombed. The footage from inside clearly shows Greg walk in, go to the back lockers, go to the information desk, then leave right before the blast. The ones from the outside aren't quite as useful. They aren't positioned in the best way, but it shows some of the parking lot."

We watch the footage from the camera until the stomach-turning moment that captures the explosion. I'm thankful the cameras don't have audio. Seeing the blast of light and the building turn to shrapnel is enough without having to hear it.

"Did they ever figure out how the explosion happened? Where the device was?" Dean asks.

"No," I tell him. "But I know a lot of people think Greg carried it into the station in the bag he's holding."

"But you don't believe that," he says.

"No. The bag doesn't look like it's holding much if anything and investigators on the scene were skeptical the source of the explosion was the lockers. There's not enough damage, and the direction of the blast overpressure is off. Which means the explosive was located somewhere else in the building."

"And you think Catch Me is responsible for it," Dean acknowledges.

"I'm sure of it. It was the first message he sent me; I just didn't realize it yet. What I don't understand is Greg's part in it. It seems disconnected. Like the two incidences overlap, but aren't the same thing," I tell him.

"Like the camera in Greg's room," Sam says.

"Exactly. Catch Me and my uncle have something to do with each other. They're linked in some way, but they aren't the same person, and I'm still convinced they aren't working together. Like I said, they are orbiting each other. Greg was with my uncle at the time of the bombing. And Catch Me obviously knew he was going to be there. If he didn't, he wouldn't have been able to manipulate Mary Preston into creating the video he sent me a clip of that shows Greg leaving something at the information desk for me. And that alone tells me Greg didn't know about the explosion. If he knew he was walking into the bus station to set off a bomb, why would he leave something at the desk for me?"

We watch through the security footage a couple more times, but none of us find a champagne-colored sedan in the parking lot.

"What else do you have?" Sam asks.

"Well, I'm actually not all that surprised to not see the car at the bus station. He's far too conscientious to just drive into the lot when he's going to be planting an explosive. Not only does he not want to be seen, but he wants to be able to get the hell away, so he doesn't

THE GIRL AND THE DEADLY END

become another statistic in his own spectacle. That's why I asked Eric to dig up the footage from the security cameras at the surrounding businesses. They haven't proven very important in the investigation, but I think it's because he didn't know what to look for. The investigators couldn't see the bus station clearly, so they weren't able to see anybody going into it or coming out, which seems like they don't see anything at all. But I want to see if we do," I say.

"Where's this?" Dean asks.

"The bus station is on a corner. There's a large main street facing the bus terminals and a smaller street to the side where the doors are. This camera is from across the main street, on a baseball stadium. It mostly shows the gates, but you can see some of the road turning into the bus station up here," I explain, pointing to the upper part of the screen.

The vantage point isn't perfect. We can't see the whole vehicle at any point, but we can see some of each car that turns down the road and even less of it as it moves into the parking lot. I don't see the champagne car, but on the third time watching through the footage, something else stands out to me.

I minimize the screen and pull up a different folder from my desktop.

"What are you doing?" Sam asks. "Did you see something?"

"Maybe," I say. "This is all the information Eric was able to give me about Mary Preston and the ongoing investigation into how she got involved with all of this. Right here, it says she drove her own vehicle to the bus station that day. It was found parked in the lot. A white SUV with red spinners on her wheels and a big red decal, advertising her website. You don't see a whole bunch of cars with spinners these days, let alone pulling into a bus station parking lot. Now, look."

Going back to the footage from the camera, I rewind it a few seconds back and point to the screen as a flash of red and white moves across the very top and disappears into the parking lot.

"How can we be sure he always drives the same car?" Dean points out. "If he doesn't want anyone knowing what he's up to, would he actually bring his own car to the hospital? Or to a bombing?"

"Yes," I nod without hesitation. "He chose a car that blends in with anything. As long as the plate isn't visible, it could belong to anyone. So, he makes sure the plate isn't seen. He parked so far out in that lot at the hospital; we barely caught sight of the car at all. And I haven't seen it here. But the big thing that convinces me he doesn't do that is that he wants to go unnoticed. When he's not coming up with new and interesting ways to torture me, he presumably lives a normal life. It would seem suspicious to anyone who knows him if he was changing cars all the time. Staying in his own car is the most streamlined option."

"Did you see that?" Sam asks.

"See what?"

He moves closer, leaning around me to point at the screen. "Right there. You can barely see it, but a white SUV with a red decal is parked right at the very edge of the lot, right there."

I look closer and see the hint of red just beneath the branches of a tree behind the sign for the bus station.

"You're right," I tell him.

"Is there more footage?" Dean asks. "Another camera that shows that corner of the lot?"

"I have one more piece. It's from the building across the side street. During the investigation, it was helpful because it showed how the explosion affected this part of the building and the direction of the blast."

The last video only plays for a few seconds before we notice the red and white flash come around the corner. It's not the whole thing, but enough to see its definitely Mary Preston's car.

"There's the car," Sam points out.

"And there's Mary," I say as legs appear walking around to the back of the SUV. She steps to the side, and slightly more of her shows up on the screen. "She's getting something out of her trunk."

"Who's that?" Dean asks.

The side of a figure approaches at a diagonal from the direction of the bus station.

"It's a man," I say. "It looks like he's stopping to talk to Mary."

My hands twitch with frustration, wanting to be able to reach into the image on the screen and move the camera so it will show more. As it is, I can only see that there is a man standing near Mary behind her car. He seems large enough to loom over her, but Mary doesn't seem uncomfortable. Her body language is relaxed as she pulls her luggage out of her trunk. She makes a move toward the station, and the man shifts just enough for me to catch a glimpse of dark hair just touching the top of his shoulder. He disappears out of view, and Mary heads for the station.

I quickly close that footage and bring up the one from the baseball field again. The bottom half of a man walks into view, coming from the parking lot.

"Is that him?" Dean asks.

"The boots are the same," I note. We keep watching. For a brief moment, he is fully in view as he walks onto the sidewalk heading down the main road. I quickly pause the feed. "There he is."

"Where do you think he's going?" Sam asks.

I shrug. "Any number of places. There's a moving truck rental place next door. A convenience store. A bit down the road, there are neighborhoods."

"And there's no footage from any of those?"

"No. But maybe Eric can get some. A lot of these places use cloud-based cameras now, so the footage should still be accessible."

I have no idea who the man is, but I want to find out. If nothing else, he talked to Mary before she went into the doomed building. I'd like to find out what they talked about and if he saw anything else.

CHAPTER SIXTEEN

"Tell me about your mother," I ask Dean a little while later as I pull a slice of pizza out of the cardboard delivery box onto a plate.

We are waiting for Eric to get back to me about any footage that might be available from further down on the street. He didn't seem terribly optimistic about the prospects when I asked him about it. It's been several months now, and even if the footage was saved on the cloud, it's possible the business owners deleted it or don't pay for access to longer-term storage and retrieval. But he said he would try, and that's as much as I can ask. Only now, it leaves us sitting around waiting, which hovers very close to the top of my list of least favorite things. I'm right on the edge, tense and sharply aware, just waiting for something to happen.

That's not an unusual feeling here. After my father left, that was my predominant state of being for a long time. I constantly waited for something. I wasn't even entirely sure what it was I was waiting for. At first, it was for him to show back up. Then it was just to get a phone call from him or a postcard, something to give me an indication that he was alive, and I would see him again. That turned into a simmering sense of anxiety and fear that came from wondering why he left, and if it wasn't actually on his own volition. Maybe he was running from something, and whatever it was would show up here.

But all that eventually faded as the months turned into years. I learned how to make peace with the tension, to not let it rule my every waking moment. But now it's back. The uncomfortable feeling of wondering and waiting and wanting to be ready but not knowing how is threatening to take over my mind.

I have to distract myself. There's no telling how long the wait will be before Eric calls back or something changes, and the game starts up again. Ever since Dean first told me about his mother and we made the disturbing link to what I convinced myself was a recurring nightmare, I've wondered about his mother, and how deep that link actually is. He talked about my father, and now we know my mother was instrumental in the rescue of his mother, but all this is yet more confusing puzzle pieces I can't quite fit. Yet more things my parents never told me about.

"I've already told you pretty much everything," he says.

"What was her name?" I asked.

"Natalia," he tells me.

"That's pretty," I say.

"I never liked it much," he admits.

"Why not?"

"It sounds too young if that makes sense. I wanted her to sound more like a mother. To sound more nurturing and... I don't know, more like other mothers. Maybe because most of the time she didn't act very motherly. I thought maybe if she sounded more like a mother, it would help. Now that I'm an adult, that sounds ridiculous and selfish."

"No, it doesn't," I reassure him. "I think all of us have things we come up with about our parents when we're young and they don't always make sense to other people. Why do you say she wasn't very motherly? You seem to adore her."

"I do," Dean says. "Her death ripped me apart. I love my mother. But everything she went through when she was younger really messed her up. Growing up in Russia wasn't easy. She came here with the hopes of having a better life and being able to help her family. But she, like far too many other women, got wrapped up with the wrong man, and he made her life a living hell. When she escaped, the only thing she took with her was her life. And she barely had that."

"How long was that before you were born?" I ask.

"About two years," he says. He gives me a knowing look over the slice of pizza he's bringing to his lips. "He wasn't my father."

Savoring the indulgent combination of spicy pepperoni and sweet pineapple against the richness of a thick layer of cheese, I finish my first bite and swallow it as I nod.

"I figured as much. You said you didn't know your father. I assumed your mother wouldn't escape from a man only to go back to him long enough to have a baby," I tell him.

I realize after I say it how judgmental it sounds, but he doesn't acknowledge it.

"What happened to your mother's ex-husband?" Sam asks.

He's already made it through a slice and is reaching for another. It doesn't surprise me. I've seen the man eat pizza before and it's always an impressive endeavor. He can lap me by a couple of slices and still be eating when I'm stuffed full. My working theory is he doesn't even taste the first slice.

"He was arrested," Dean tells him. "Thanks to you, Emma."

I have another bite in my mouth, and I swallow it so quickly I nearly choke.

"Me?" I ask. "What did I have to do with anything? I wasn't even born when my mother helped yours."

"I know, but my mother once told me she was strong enough to get away from her husband because someone was there to help her and strong enough to stay away because that person stayed around. I can only imagine she was talking about your mother. But the one thing she didn't immediately do was submit a police report and press charges. She didn't even want to file for divorce. Not that she wanted to stay married to him, obviously. But the idea of getting the police and the government and everything else tangled up in it was completely overwhelming to her. But then she said her friend got pregnant."

"My mother got pregnant with me," I say.

Dean nods.

"Watching your mother go through pregnancy and seeing how happy your father was waiting for you showed Mom what being in a relationship is really supposed to be like. It made her have hope that maybe one day she'd find someone, and we could all have a family together. That's when she had your mother help her file for divorce. She convinced Mom to ask for an emergency divorce without the necessity for her ex-husband to be in the same room at any point. She told the judge how he treated her, and he not only granted the emergency divorce but advised her to file criminal charges. She did and he ended up in prison with an eighteen-year sentence. And soon after, she met someone and ended up pregnant."

"Was she in a relationship with him? Your father?" I ask. "I'm sorry. Is that too personal?"

"No," he says. "It's fine. I honestly don't know if she thought she was in a relationship with him or not. It's possible they just went on a date or two. But the few times I heard her talk about him, she always said he was so charming and made her feel beautiful. But then he was gone. Just like that. It really sent her spiraling. During a particularly difficult time when I was younger, she told me him leaving her was almost worse than the end of her relationship with her husband, because it was so sudden and unexpected. It left her feeling worthless and broken. It reminded her of how much her husband tore her down, and every time he told her no man would ever love her the way he did. It led her to drinking, and even when she wasn't drinking, she had PTSD from the abuse. She'd go into these phases."

His voice trails off, and I lean toward him slightly to encourage him to keep going.

"What kind of phases?" I ask.

"She wouldn't want to leave the house. Sometimes she wouldn't want to leave her bed. Sometimes she cried and shook for hours. Other times it was like she wasn't there at all. Her eyes were open, but she didn't react to anything or anyone. She just stared at the wall. I had to learn very young not only to take care of myself but of her, too."

"I don't understand why no one was there to help you. If my mother did help get Natalia away from her ex, why would she just abandon you?" I ask. "You said Murdock didn't come to help you until after your mother died."

"I don't think she abandoned us. I think it was the other way around," he tells me.

"What do you mean?" I ask.

"I have some memories of being much younger. She would make me go to my room when people came over. It happened pretty regularly, a few times a month. It never seemed like they were just coming over to hang out or it was a party. They were there for a reason, but I was never allowed to meet them or see them. Things were always a little better after those visits. Mom was calmer and we had a little more money. When I was about six, she told me to go to my room, but it wasn't like the other times. She'd just gotten off the phone, and it was like she was surprised. I listened at the door, and when the person got there, she greeted them, there was a little bit of a muffled conversation, then she shouted 'no'. I heard a struggle and was scared. After a few seconds, I opened the door to go help her, but she had already slammed the door and was putting the chain lock on. That night, we started packing and moved. We didn't have any more of those visitors."

"And you didn't see who the person was?"

"No. Things got a little bit better after your mother died, but I still didn't see or hear about any of them. It wasn't until those four days she disappeared that there was anyone actually there to help," he says. "Then, about a year before her death, we moved into the apartment."

"In the same complex where I was staying with my father," I say.

"I had no idea," he tells me.

I lean back against the couch to think through what he just told me.

"When your mother was gone for those four days, you said she left a note."

"Right, she said she would be back."

"So, you didn't call the police," I confirm.

Dean shakes his head and pries a piece of pepperoni off his slice of pizza.

"No."

"I still can't believe your mother disappeared, and you didn't think it would be a good idea to let the police know," Sam says.

"The police never helped my mother."

"Not until they put her scumbag ex into jail," Sam snaps.

"After he almost killed her, and she had to run. I grew up knowing if the police ever knew about Mom's problems; the only thing they would do is take me from her. There was no way I was going to let that happen," Dean retorts.

"I don't think she disappeared," I say. "It was planned. Strategic. She left you a note, that's part of it but think about it. You didn't call the police or let anyone know she was missing. But then Murdock showed up. You didn't know him, but he was able to convince you your mother trusted him enough to watch out for you. Natalia didn't just walk away. She went on a mission."

CHAPTER SEVENTEEN

MARIYA

THIRTY YEARS AGO...

When she was young, dreaming of the life that waited for her at the end of childhood, this was what she imagined. Everyone had their dreams for her. Their expectations and demands. From her parents it was love and aspiration. They wanted better for their little girl. They wanted more.

From others, it was arrogance. They weren't dreaming for her. When they thought of her, she wasn't a person, but a commodity. They thought only of what she could do for them and how it could benefit their own lives. They believed in their superiority in their entitlement to her. They wrapped it in a pretty bow, draped it in satin, and surrounded it with music, but the intention was still lurking underneath. They only wanted her for the body she was born with. They could mold her into their perfect vision. Train her from the time she was able to stand to become exactly what they wanted her to be.

People would come from everywhere to see her, they told her. They would adore her. But it was never about her. Her name was little more than the label on a product. No one sitting up in the velvet seats carrying on in applause truly cared about the blood pumping through her heart or the thoughts in her mind. They didn't care about her eyes or her fingerprints. The only thing that kept her apart from others that mattered to them was the way the music formed itself in her bones and muscles and moved her across the well-worn wood.

It was a proud tradition. Those were some of the earliest words she ever knew. She was taught in the old ways. Ways honored so they wouldn't be lost. When anyone in the world thought of ballet, they thought of Russia, she was told. That was something to be proud of.

She wanted to be proud. She wanted to feel that rush of excitement and devotion she saw in the men and women who taught her. They had a passion she never had. It was what made the men leap so high it looked like they were flying. What made the women float like rose petals in their partners' hands. They were born with that. It was in them from before their first breath. Those dancers inherited their passion through the generations, the same way she inherited the blond of her hair and the length of her legs.

But she did not inherit that passion. She didn't love what she did. She wanted to. She wanted to be proud of the heritage that made her name known. She wanted more than anything to look out over the audience and find joy and fulfillment in their adulation. She wanted to lose herself under the lights, the stage, the rising curtain, the delicate precision, the joyous frenzy, the twirls, and tiptoes, and leaps, and lifts. The low curtsy to welcome cheers and applause washing over her.

It was her place to be a dream shared by all of them; a painting brought to life. She was a confection of softness and light when they looked at her. She tried to remember that. But she knew the blood in her shoes, the bruises from falls. She knew the tiny pinprick pains from her hair combed sharply back and pinned in place. The rigorous hours of practice. The tragedy of her companions, her friends, suffering from injuries that ruined their lives forever. They would never dance again. They were simply discarded.

It wasn't for her. She did it for her parents for as long as she could. But it wasn't what she wanted. There was so much more in the world, and she knew it. She could feel what else existed beyond the studio and stage. That's what she dreamed of. Moonlight on her skin rather than stage lights. Bare feet rather than pointe shoes. The gaze of one man rather than a sea of eyes.

When she met Ian he showed her that type of life could exist for her. The possibility was there. All she had to do was chase after it. He brought her into his world and gave her what her parents truly wanted for her. And what she wanted for herself. A life that was better. A life that was hers.

He would be home soon. Five days without him felt so long. She was used to him having to leave and the time it took away from her. It wasn't something she would ever complain about or try to fight against. What he did was important, just like what she did was important, and he never tried to keep her away from the days she had to leave for that. It made the time they had together more precious. The love and affection they couldn't give to each other in those days when they were apart was distilled down into when they could be together, making every one of those seconds more valuable.

She wanted to stay awake and wait for him, but there was no way of knowing exactly when he would get back. It could be tonight; it could be tomorrow afternoon. At least she knew she would be in his arms by dinner the next day. He had promised. And he never broke a promise to her.

She left the window open to let in the freshness of the August night. She took a shower and dressed in a gauzy nightgown before slipping into bed. Crisp, newly cleaned sheets, felt soft and cool against her skin, lulling her quickly to sleep.

The sleep didn't stay with her long. It felt like her eyes were closed for only a few minutes when the other side of the bed dipped down, and warmth cradled her body. The darkness of the room sharpened her other senses. His touch sent shivers along her skin. He leaned toward her and touched his lips to the side of her neck. She tried to speak to him, but he silenced her with a kiss.

He gently rolled her onto her back and settled over her, the weight of his body pressing her down into the mattress and surrounding her.

She could disappear into this. She could melt into the enveloping presence of him and not think of anything else.

And that was just what she did. She thought of nothing else and let him fade away the emptiness of the five days they were apart. They didn't matter now. She fell asleep in his arms and knew nothing until morning.

It wasn't a kiss or even the shift of his body that woke her up. Early sunlight came through the window, glowing on her eyes. She vaguely shed her layers of sleep enough to become aware of the sound of a car rumbling into the driveway. Her eyes snapped open. Was Ian leaving again? He just got home.

The other side of the bed was cold when she felt it. That didn't make sense. He couldn't have gotten up that long ago. Slipping into her bathrobe, she rushed across the room. There was no smell of soap, no feeling of lingering steam from a shower coming from the open bathroom door. The closet door was still closed, a dress she'd hung from it the day before undisturbed.

She got to the window just in time to hear the driver's side door close and see Ian walk around to the trunk. He opened it and reached inside for his suitcase. Confusion twisted in her mind. As if he could feel her eyes on him, he looked up and caught sight of her in the window. A bright smile crossed his face, and he waved.

"Hello, darling," he called. "I've missed you. You're up early. I thought I was going to get a chance to surprise you."

Her stomach turned as searing heat clawed down the back of her neck. By the time Ian got inside, she was in the bathroom, soaking in scalding water and scrubbing away any of the touches that might have lingered on her skin.

CHAPTER EIGHTEEN

NOW

Dean sets his piece of pizza down and wipes his hands off on a napkin as he stares at me.

"You mean you think she was helping your mother," he says.

"Yes," I tell him. "When I was younger, right up until the day she died, we traveled around all the time. We moved constantly. There would be stretches of time when my father was gone and then stretches of time when my mother was gone. My mother being gone wasn't as common, but it always seemed that when we moved somewhere new, she would go away for several days, or had meetings or appointments. Then when it was done, we might settle down for a little while, but then we were scooped up and moved again. I always assumed it was my father's CIA work. And I'm sure some of it was. But now I know we were moving, and she was leaving to help the women she was rescuing."

"What does that have to do with my mother?" Dean asks, suddenly sounding almost defensive, like I'm threatening the already tenuous grasp he has on his mother's life and what it all means.

"Maybe she was helping my mother with one of her missions. I can't even imagine what these women were going through when they needed to be rescued. I can't even wrap my head around being in a place in life where you feel so hopeless that the only option is to leave everything behind. To have to reach out to someone to help you. Can you imagine the fear?"

"Of course I can. I saw it in my mother's face every day. Every time she watched the news and they talked about a woman getting attacked, or she saw surveillance footage of someone who looked even slightly like her ex-husband, I saw the terror all over again."

"Then you understand why it would be hard. That level of fear doesn't come from feeling like you have freedom or a life worth living. The most dangerous days of an abused woman's life are the ones right before and right after she leaves. Statistically, that's when most of them are killed. Their partner finds out what they're planning, or they come home, and she's gone. They know they've lost control, and they destroy the woman who angered and offended them. For some women, that terror is enough to keep them from leaving. They would rather just stay with the brutality and fear they already live with on a daily basis than have to try to make their own way in the world while also coping with the fear of losing their lives. As much as I would like to think that the women offered help by the Spice organization would be eager to accept it, my professional experience tells me it's not that simple," I tell him.

"Mine too," he sighs. "I've been hired by those monsters to follow women and find out if they are planning on leaving and where they are going. Or they tried, anyway. I would always tip the women off and do what I could to cover their tracks."

I nod. "They need all the help they can get. They need to know they are safe. Tell me something. After those four days when your mother was gone, did she get better? Did she have as many of the phases you were talking about?"

"No."

"Because she helped someone else. She got that reminder of what she escaped from and the future she had in front of her. Those four days were spent saving another woman's life," I tell him. "It must be that."

THE GIRL AND THE DEADLY END

"Is there any way to find out what she did or where she went? Records? Anything?" he asks.

"I just found out about this organization," I remind him. "I didn't even know it existed, much less that my mother was a part of it. My father arranged to have all of her things moved after she died, and I don't remember ever seeing anything like files or records."

My phone alerts me to a new message, and I stand up to get it. It's Eric.

"Eric got footage from the convenience store down the block from the bus station," I announce.

I try to temper my excitement, to cool the shock of optimism. I remind myself that it doesn't mean we actually found anything or have more information than we did, to begin with. We still don't know who the man is, or if he saw anything useful at the station. All I can hope is that this footage will show more of his face, and we can recognize him.

Pulling up the footage, I sit down between the two men so we can all watch it. The camera angle isn't perfect. It's more like a time-lapse, so the video is uneven and jerking, but it's something. We watch the sidewalk carefully, and sure enough, the man appears on the screen.

"He pulled his hood up," Sam points out. "We can't see his face."

"No, but that's definitely him. Those are the same boots, the same pants. He's the same size," I say.

The man doesn't seem in a rush or at all concerned as he makes his way toward the building.

"Where is he going?" Dean mutters.

He's not heading toward the doors or the gas pumps but moving around to the side. I glance at the time clock ticking by on the screen.

"The explosion is going to happen any second," I note.

My body braces. I know it's coming, yet there's still anxiety. There's no sound, but at the exact moment I know it's going to come, there's a flash of light at the upper corner of the screen. People scatter. Some run in the direction of the explosion while others move inside the store as fast as they can. I keep my eyes locked on where the man stepped off-screen. It takes a few seconds, but he steps back out into view.

"He's completely calm," Sam notes. "He's not reacting. Everybody else is doing something. They're running around or staring. They're on the phone. Look, they're all reacting to what just happened, but he's not. It's like he has no idea what just happened."

"Or he knows exactly what happened," I counter.

"Because he knew it was going to," Dean agrees.

"He's going toward the parking area," Sam points out. "There are only a few minutes until the emergency responders show up. He knows he's got to get the hell out of there."

The camera covers most of the parking area, cutting off only the edges of the outermost cars at the edge of the visible row. But that doesn't make a difference. The man walks out of sight again, disappearing around to the other side of the building.

"You don't have footage from any cameras there?" Dean asks.

"This is all Eric sent me," I tell him. "Wait. Look."

A champagne sedan glides into view and stops at the entrance to the parking lot, waiting calmly for people running by. It's a still, steady moment, like the car exists in a totally different realm of reality. All around it, people are frantic. Cars speed down the street. Lights of emergency vehicles start flashing at the edges of the screen. But the nondescript compact sits patiently at the entrance, the turn signal ticking, until the way is clear, then moves smoothly and easily onto the road.

"Turn it back, look for a license plate," Sam says.

We watch the footage again, but it's too grainy to make out the plate number.

"Damn it," I growl. "Why bother having cameras that don't show the details that actually matter?"

"It did," Sam offers. "It showed him."

"We just have to figure out who he is."

The video is far from conclusive. It shows little more than a hooded man responding to an emergency situation with indifference,

THE GIRL AND THE DEADLY END

and then an admittedly common as hell car drive away. But it's enough to create a link. It's enough to make me want to know more.

A call coming in breaks up the video, and a number appears across the screen.

"It's the hospital," Sam says.

I get to my feet, stepping away from the couch as I answer.

"Hello?"

My heart is in my throat as I wait for the doctor to tell me Greg took a turn for the worse or security was breached again. Both as another human being and as a person I have a history with, I don't want to think of him suffering anymore. Or losing his life. But it's more than that. He has information locked inside him. Secrets and details only he can tell. I need to hear them to know what happened.

"Emma?"

The voice on the other end of the line cracks, rising barely above a whisper, but the chill it creates lifts the hairs on my arms and the back of my neck. I reach out for Sam, and he jumps up to take my hand, pulling me close against him.

"Greg?"

CHAPTER NINETEEN

"I told him what happened when he was mumbling. He wanted to be the one to call you," Amelia calls after me as I burst out of the elevator and onto the secure hospital floor.

She was waiting for us outside the elevator and fell into step behind me as I rush past her toward Greg's room.

"How long has he been awake?" I ask.

"About forty-five minutes before he called you," she says.

"Why didn't you call me?"

"The doctors insisted on checking him over and making sure he was in good condition."

"And?"

"He looks good. All considering. He was very eager to talk to you."

"He doesn't sound great," I say. "His voice sounds really rough."

"The ventilator often causes a little bit of temporary damage to the throat. There's some evidence of minor throat injuries from whatever happened to him before he was found. But it's not permanent. He should be back to normal with continued healing and practice speaking," she tells me.

I get to the door to his room and pause. I've been here before. In this moment of hesitation and uncertainty before walking in. Only this time, I know what's on the other side of the curtain. This time I know he's awake. Hopefully, he's gotten through the worst of it. It would seem that after spending the last few days in the room with him, it wouldn't seem so nerve-wracking to go in, but nervousness flutters inside me. In all the time he was gone, and even more once he reappeared on my front lawn unconscious, I let myself think about what it would be like to actually talk to him again. All my focus was on just hoping he would survive. But now I have to navigate how different my life is now then it was the last time we saw each other.

Taking a breath, I open the door and push the curtain aside. In that second, I'm in two segments of my life. It's suddenly two years ago, before Feathered Nest, before Sherwood. I'm trying to understand my relationship with Greg and what it means. I don't want to be in this place, wondering if he's going to try to explain away our breakup and try again. But Sam steps up behind me, and the warmth of his hand on my hip keeps me anchored here.

Greg is looking toward the window when we walk in, but he turns to me as I step up to the side of the bed. Even looking less severe with healing, the bruises and cuts on his face change his appearance. It's hard to look at him. I know it's him. There isn't a question about that, but it's still difficult to process seeing him awake and responding to me after two years of questions and wondering.

"Hi, Emma," he whispers, not trying to force his voice louder like he did on the phone.

I step up closer.

"Hi, Greg," I smile sadly. "It's good to see you awake."

I want to ask how he's feeling, but the words feel like feathers in my mouth. Useless and flighty. Just something people say to fill space and acknowledge set situations. Instead, I pull a chair over and sit down. Maybe this should be one of those times I push my career aside and try to think purely as one person reaching out to another, but I can't. When I look at Greg, I'm relieved he's awake and healing. I don't want him to suffer any more pain or experience any ill effects after

THE GIRL AND THE DEADLY END

this. But I also can't wait. I can't use up any more of the time I have waiting for information, searching for details.

"Greg, how did you get here? Two years ago... what happened?"

"The nurse told me there was a picture," he croaks.

I nod. "Do you know how they found you?"

"Not much. Just that I've been out for a while."

"You were wrapped in plastic. There were pictures wrapped with you and he…"

Emotion hits me suddenly, but I fight to keep it out of my voice, not wanting to cause any more stress and upset in this already difficult situation. "He dumped you out of a car into my yard."

He drew in a breath. I can almost see his mind grinding, churning through the memories of what happened to him over the last two years.

"Do you have the picture?" he asks.

The original is in the investigation files. It didn't occur to me Amelia would tell him about it without telling him what was in it. I take out my phone and search through the messages for the one Bellamy sent to me the day they found Greg.

"There are others, but this is the one they showed me."

I turn the screen to him, and he takes the phone from my hand, staring with a stony jaw at the image of him and my uncle sitting in the car.

"What are the other ones?" he asks.

"Your injuries, another of the two of you together, one of an open grave."

He nods slowly, then hands me the phone.

"Do you remember the night you were working late, and I got upset because we weren't going to get to the restaurant on time?" he asks.

"Yes," I tell him. "You went to pick some food up for us."

"Yes," Greg nods. "That's when I met him." He nods toward the phone. "He was in the parking deck. I couldn't believe what I was seeing. There, standing in front of me, was the mythical Ian Griffin."

"Greg," I say painfully, shaking my head as I try to figure out how I'm going to explain this all to him.

"I know," he says before I can even continue.

"You do?" I ask.

"That wasn't your father. I didn't know it at the time. Really, I didn't. I had heard so much about him and how incredible his career was. It was such an honor just to meet him, then when he said," Greg pauses, tilting his head back and closing his eyes as he seems to concentrate on taking in a breath and swallowing.

"You don't have to keep going," I tell him. "You can take a break."

He lifts his head, shaking it adamantly.

"No, I need to tell you this. I've been waiting two years for this."

"Alright," I say. "Go ahead."

"He told me the reason no one had seen him in so long was he was deep undercover doing extremely dangerous, highly classified work. He wasn't able to tell you what he was doing or where he was going because he needed to protect you. So I wasn't allowed to tell you I saw him. He told me he came to recruit me; that he'd been watching my career closely and was impressed, so he wanted me to work with him. He had an organization called Leviathan, and I had been chosen to apprentice under him. Of course, I agreed. Then he told me I would have to leave essentially my entire life behind. I would have to end my relationship with you and just disappear the way he had. It felt like an impossible decision."

"No, it didn't," I tell him. "And that's alright. This is everything you've ever worked for. I understand why you would immediately jump on the opportunity."

"Leviathan..." Sam muses, sending a meaningful look to Dean and me.

"I honestly believed it wouldn't be long before I was able to tell you what was going on and bring your father back into your life. But then I realized there was something else going on. He wasn't the man I thought he was," he says.

"How long did it take you to realize it?"

"Longer than I'd like to admit. There are things I did I will never be able to atone for, things I participated in I thought were for good, but I will never be able to forgive myself for doing," he tells me, his voice dropping even further.

I reach out and rest my hand on his. "You don't need to be forgiven. All of us have to do things in this career that we regret. That's part of this life. You have to remember that what you do is for the greater good. Sacrifices need to be made."

"Not these kinds of sacrifices. The only sacrifice I was fully willing to make, I didn't have to."

"What do you mean?" I ask.

"Did you find the signature in the guest book at the funeral home?" he asks.

I'm surprised to hear him bring it up now, but I nod.

"Yes. How did you do that?" I ask.

"I didn't. But I had someone do it for me. In case…" he draws in a breath. "In case I didn't get the chance to talk to you again, I needed you to know I tried. I needed you to start searching. Did you get the book?"

"The guest book you signed?"

"No, the one older one. He said he signed it for your mother."

I shake my head. "No. Bellamy is the one who found the signature. They wouldn't talk to her." I feel like we're sliding away from what's important, and I can already see Greg getting tired. I lean closer to him. "Greg, what is my uncle's name? Who is he?"

"Lotan," he says, his voice dropping down to a whisper again. "I only know Lotan."

I swallow hard and glance back at Sam and Dean, who nod.

"Greg, I need you to…" I start, but he suddenly takes my hand, stopping me.

It looks like he's fighting to stay awake, and I'm sure the medication they still have pumping through him to manage his pain doesn't make that easy.

"Emma, he's coming for you."

"When?" Sam demands. "What do you know?"

Greg's eyes are slowly closing.

"He says it's time you know the truth. You were taken from him. You can't let him take you."

"What do you mean?" I ask, my heart pounding, so the base of my throat shakes, and bile stings the back of my tongue. "What are you talking about? What truth?"

"He wants you first. You were what he always wanted. Then the other. His children together to reign."

CHAPTER TWENTY

The words are like ice down my shoulders and into my chest.

"What are you talking about?" I ask desperately. "Greg, what do you mean?"

I stand and lean over him, speaking directly into his face, trying to rouse him again.

"Emma," Sam says, taking my hips and trying to pull me backwards away from the bed.

"What did you just say?" I demand. "What do you mean?"

Amelia comes into the room, forcing back the curtain and rushing to the bedside.

"Emma, please," she scolds. "You're disturbing the other patients. He's still heavily medicated, and he's going to need to sleep. He'll wake up again later, but you'll have to be more restrained."

I step up close to the nurse, getting my face to within inches of hers.

"Back off," I growl.

"Emma," Sam warns, yanking me back and pulling me to the other side of the room. "You have to stop. If you want any chance at all of figuring out what's going on, you need to calm down. She could have you removed and not let you back in here. Take a breath."

"Did you hear what he said?" I ask, lowering my voice so Amelia can't overhear me.

"Yes," he says. "I did. But it's not going to do you any good screaming at an unconscious man. When he wakes up, you can talk to him and find out what he meant."

"I can't wait until he wakes up," I snap. "He said my uncle is coming for me because he wants his children to be together."

"You need to calm down and think clearly," Sam tells me. "Think about what you're saying. You know that isn't true. You didn't even know he exists. How could he be your father?"

Realization hits me. My legs suddenly feel like they can't support my weight. Sam notices my knees buckling and takes hold of my upper arms, leading me over to the couch and letting me sit. He sits down beside me, and I read his eyes.

"He's not," I say. Reaching into my pocket, I take out my phone and call Eric. "I need you to put a rush on a DNA comparison test for me. Two people. I need it done as soon as possible. Let the crime lab know it involves a rape." I take a breath. "And possibly murder."

"You got it," says Eric.

Sam is staring at me with questions in his eyes when I get off the phone.

"Rape?" he asks. "Who was raped?"

"My mother," I tell him. "Think about what we found in her medical records. When she was in Feathered Nest, she went to the Women's Center at the hospital and got the morning after pill. But a little over than a month later, she was pregnant with me. Why would she take precautions to prevent a pregnancy one month and then happily welcome another just a few weeks later? Unless it was because the first potential pregnancy would have been with someone she didn't want to have a child with?"

Sam's face went pale.

"He wouldn't have even had to attack her," he muses. "In the dark, it's possible he could have convinced her he was Ian."

I nod. "Exactly. But she would have figured it out. And as soon as she realized what happened to her, she would do anything she could to avoid giving birth to a child that would inextricably link her to her husband's brother. That picture we found of the two of them. We both thought it was my parents, not just because of his appearance, but also the way he was looking at her. He was obsessed."

"But who is the second person?"

"Dean," I tell him.

Sam looks over at Dean, who turns widened eyes to me.

"Me?" He furrows his brow and takes a step closer. "Why me? Why would you need my DNA?"

"Do you have that picture of your mother you showed me at the cabin?"

"I don't have the paper, but I can find it." He searches through his phone for a few seconds, then shows Sam the image of his mother smiling. "That's her."

Sam looks at me, and I give a single nod.

"You see it, too, don't you?"

"See what?" Dean asks.

"Have you ever seen a picture of my mother?" I ask him.

When he says he hasn't, I do a quick search through my phone and show him.

"They look so much alike," he notes.

"Which is exactly why I always thought I was having a nightmare about walking into that apartment and finding my mother dead. It was your mother. Like I said, that man is obsessed with my mother. When she wouldn't run away with him, he had to find a substitute. From the moment I saw you, I thought there was something familiar about you. But now I realize it's not that you are familiar, it's that you look like someone who is. Will you take the test with me?"

He nods but doesn't say anything. A few minutes later, Eric calls back and gives us instructions for where to go to get the test. The swab itself can be done right here in the hospital, then a tech from the crime lab will come to collect the samples and run the comparison test.

Dean and I go to the appointed room. The test itself only takes a few seconds, and as we walk out, he looks at me.

"What now?" he asks.

"Now, we wait."

Bellamy calls as we're making our way back up to Greg's room.

"Are you still at the hospital?" she asks, sounding breathless.

"Yes. I was just heading back to Greg's room. Why? What's going on? Is something wrong?" I ask.

"No. I just need to see you. You're not going to believe what just showed up at my house," she says. "I'll be up there in twenty minutes."

My head spins as I make my way back to Greg's room, where Sam waits for us. I didn't want to risk Greg waking back up and us not being there. He stands up from the couch when we walk in.

"So?"

"The results could take a little while. They'll rush it as much as they can, but the labs are notoriously busy," I tell him.

"Then what's wrong?" he frowns, coming up and taking my hands.

He squeezes them, and the warmth of his skin against mine makes me aware of how cold mine are.

"Bellamy just called. She says she got something in the mail today and needs to show it to me now. She's on her way over here."

The expression on his face exudes the same anxiety I'm feeling. I can't imagine what she could have gotten that would be so urgent. Unless she's become the next unwitting player in Catch Me's game.

"I'm going to get coffee," Sam says. "Do you want some?"

I nod and sit down on the couch. He offers some to Dean, who nods, but it seems like he doesn't quite hear Sam. When Sam leaves the room, Dean walks over to the window and stares out over the city. I want to say something to him, but I don't know what. It's impossible for me to guess or even begin to understand what he might be thinking or feeling right now. I'm already struggling with my own thoughts. The new level of pure disgust and hatred I have for the man who shared my father's childhood and at least part of his adulthood.

Sam comes back, balancing three cups of coffee and hands them out. We sip in silence. It feels like far longer than twenty minutes when Bellamy finally comes through the door. She's carrying a large padded white envelope, and her face is bright and wind-chapped. I realize I didn't even pay attention to the weather when we were running in after Greg called. A quick glance toward the window tells me the thought I had when I saw the white sky was right. Snowflakes have begun to drift down.

I get to my feet and cross the room to her.

"What is it?" I ask.

"I didn't tell you because I thought you already had enough going on, but a few weeks ago, I got in touch with the funeral home again."

"The one in Florida?" I ask.

She nods as we make our way back over to the couch. "I told you the guy working there seemed like he was willing to talk to me but was stopped for some reason. So, I tried again. I explained I wasn't a rival or disgruntled family member. This had nothing to do with them or their business practices. But if they happened to be covering up for the mob and dabbling in money laundering and human trafficking through the use of fraudulent funeral services, my friends at the Bureau might end up wanting to pay them a visit."

"Damn, Bells. Creagan should start sending you undercover," I comment.

"We'll see. It might not have actually come to anything. But I got this in the mail today, along with a letter saying he got this out of storage. He said I could compare it to local obituary notices to prove they weren't doing anything wrong. Seems a bit sketchy in the whole personal privacy scheme of things, but I'm not going to argue with it," she tells me.

She reaches into the envelope, and the breath leaves my lungs as she pulls out a guest book.

"How did he know?" I murmur.

CHAPTER TWENTY-ONE

"I told him the date of your mother's supposed funeral," Bellamy says. "I'm sure funeral homes keep things labeled in storage."

I look over at her and have to think for a second about what she just said for it to make sense, then shake my head.

"No," I say. "That's not what I mean. I meant Greg. How did he know the guest book was coming?"

"He said it was coming?" Bellamy asks.

"Not exactly. But he mentioned it. He asked about the signature," I say.

"Of course he did. He left that for you. He wanted to make sure you found it."

I make a sound of acknowledgement, but there's a little voice in the back of my mind that tells me there's more to it than that. That man at the funeral home didn't just suddenly change his mind. Bellamy's somewhat legally ambiguous threats aside, I feel like someone's helping me.

"Or maybe my mother is just ready for this to be over and gave him a little push," I muse.

Bellamy gives me a sad smile and wraps her arm around my shoulders for a hug.

"What did Greg say about the book?" she asks.

"He asked if I found his signature, and then if I found the older book, the one my uncle signed."

"The one your uncle signed?" she tilts her head. "He was there?"

"Why 'supposed funeral'?"

I look up at Dean, almost startled by his voice.

"What?" I ask.

"Bellamy said your mother's 'supposed funeral'. What did she mean by that?"

"My mother was cremated," I explain. "In a different state. I went to the memorial service and saw her urn. But it wasn't a funeral. As far as I ever knew, there was no memorial service for her in Florida. But Bellamy went down there a few months ago to look into a couple of leads for me and found an announcement for a funeral for my mother. My father and I never attended it. I don't know why there was one in Florida."

Bellamy chimes in with her half of the story. "So I went to this funeral home and tried to get some information about it, but they wouldn't talk. The only info they gave me was that someone else had been in there just the week before asking about the same service, and he'd insisted on signing the guest book."

"That's what you were talking about when Greg asked about his signature in the other guest book," Dean acknowledges.

"Yes. We knew it was a message but couldn't figure out what it meant. Especially because he signed it with the middle name Ron. Now I know Greg didn't actually sign it, but someone he trusted did. He wanted to get my attention and make me look into her service more."

"Why would there be a grave and a casket if she was cremated somewhere else?" he asks.

"I don't know. Especially considering her urn is in my house. She was never interred in any way."

I flip through the pages of the guest book, looking at the names. Dozens pack the lines of every page, representing the lives of so many people lost. It's like looking at the charred beams left behind when a

THE GIRL AND THE DEADLY END

barn burns. You can still see what used to be, but it isn't there anymore and can never really be again.

"A couple of these names look familiar," Bellamy notes, running her fingertips down one of the pages.

"Look, this is the date that was on the announcement," I tell her, pointing to the top of the page. "It looks like someone had used a felt-tip pen to write the date in small numbers at the top of each page to keep it organized. I know some of these names. They're people my mother knew when I was younger. I don't remember much about any of them, but I know I've heard their names."

"Friends of your mother were invited to a fake funeral?" Dean asks.

"That's what it seems like happened."

"Maybe it was like people who elope and then go home and have a big wedding ceremony for their friends and family so they can feel like they witnessed the ceremony," Bellamy suggests. "Your father wanted to bring your mother to be cremated and have a smaller service, but he knew your mother's friends would want to give their respects."

"Only in a second wedding ceremony the bride and groom are actually there. They don't just prop up a wedding dress and tux and let everybody pretend," I reply. "There was a casket, and there's a grave. That's a lot to go through just so people can feel like they paid their last respects."

I scan through the next few pages, and Bellamy suddenly grabs my arm.

"Emma, look," she says, pointing at the book. "Griffin. But it's on the wrong day. He was there, but four days after her funeral."

I look at the signature, then glance at the date at the top of the page. She's right; it's marked days after the funeral service held for my mother. But there's something that stands out against the other signatures on the page. I flip back to the page with the correct date.

"No, look. Here are the signatures from the day of the funeral service," I flip back to the other page. "And these are the ones from the day he signed it. The ink is different. The ones from the day of my mother's service are blue. Every other one on the page with this signature are black. The pens are different. This is him. He signed it, but for some reason, he turned to another page."

"So no one would notice?" Bellamy offers. "Maybe he didn't want anybody seeing his name in the guest book."

"Why would it matter if anybody saw his name if he was there?"

"He left before anybody could notice him," she points out. "Don't you think her friends might find it odd to see someone who looks just like your father when they know he isn't there?"

"We know Catch Me was there," Dean muses.

"How do you know that?" Bellamy asks.

"One of the clues he left in Feathered Nest," I say, suddenly remembering it. "It was talking about Marren's roses. He said the flowers at my mother's funeral were beautiful, but he wondered why the casket seemed so light."

"They did bury a casket," Bellamy says. "The people in Florida thought they were at a real funeral."

"So, what were they burying?" Dean asks.

"I don't know, but I think we need to find out. That casket needs to be exhumed."

"You're going to have to petition the court for that," Bellamy says. "People get squeamish when it comes to digging graves up."

"I know. That's why we're going to ask Creagan to put in the request."

"Creagan?" Bellamy asks, surprised. "I thought you didn't want him to have anything to do with the case. You didn't want the Bureau to get involved."

"I don't," I admit. "But the courts tend to act a lot faster when law enforcement is greasing the wheels. A judge might go a bit slower if it was just me asking them to disinter my mother's casket because I have suspicions about the burial. But if the Bureau in conjunction with a sheriff were to put in a request as part of an ongoing investigation, we'd save a lot of time."

"What investigation?" Dean asks.

"My mother's murder. It was never solved. The official police report says she was shot multiple times, but they never found any leads about the assailants."

"Assailants? Multiple?"

"Evidence at the crime scene including footprints and inconsistencies with the blood splatter suggests there was more than one person there the night she was killed," I explain. "And I'm sure a judge will be sympathetic to the FBI wanting to further the investigation, especially with the cooperation of a sheriff who has taken a special interest in the safety of the murder victim's daughter following a series of unsolved break-ins at her home."

"And you're okay with that?" Sam asks.

"Are you?" I ask.

"Of course, I am," he agrees. "I'll do anything I can to help you. I just want to make sure you're ready. You could be tangling up a pretty tight web here, and courts don't always respond well to skirting the truth so closely."

"I said I would do what needed to be done. I'm not doing anything that isn't legitimate. Her case is cold. It does need further investigation. I have no interest in getting Creagan any more involved than he already has gotten, but some quick thinking and fancy footwork will get me what I need and still keep him from taking over control."

"Alright," he sighs. "Then let's go talk to him."

I look over at Dean.

"You coming?" I ask.

"I think I'll sit this one out. Get caught up on some work."

I nod.

"See you back at the house later?"

"Sure."

I give him a tense smile and start for the door but pause when he calls out to me.

"Emma."

"Hmm?" I turn back to him.

"What's his name?" he asks. "You saw his signature. What's his name?"

My breath slides out of my lungs, and my mouth twitches, not even wanting to say it.

"Jonah," I finally tell him.

"Jonah," he repeats softly, nodding.

"It would almost be funny if it wasn't so horrific," I say.

"What would?"

"Lotan and Leviathan. Jonah and the whale."

CHAPTER TWENTY-TWO

I didn't expect my visit to the headquarters to go quickly. It was never going to be as simple as just walking in and having a meeting with Creagan. This used to be where I spent every day working. For a few years, I saw the inside of FBI headquarters more than I did my own home. In fact, there were more nights than I like to admit that I spent on a cot in the barrack-room rather than making the drive back to my house. Especially in the midst of a difficult case, when I needed every second I could possibly juice out of the day to concentrate on untangling the clues or planning operations, it was just easier to be able to drop down for an hour or two then roll right back up than it would be to commute.

Now it's been so long since I even stepped foot in the building, and my colleagues are eager to stop me and talk. I have to be careful about what I say to each of them. Despite the FBI's record for secrecy, there's very little discretion when it comes to sharing case details with your colleagues. It's kind of an open secret. What I say to one will eventually trickle its way to others, so I have to be sure to give the exact same details and reasoning to each. It's not quite the same as juggling elaborate lies, but I feel like I'm putting the truth through a sifter. All the fine details fall away, and I offer up only the most prominent, unobtrusive facts.

I don't mention Greg. I don't know if word of him waking up has made it here yet, and even if it has, I don't want to get caught up in conversations about him. That's not why I'm here. I can't afford to get distracted. Everything I'm trying to piece together will bring the man who brutalized him to justice. But I have to find him first.

Once I get through all the unpleasant small talk, it's time to face Creagan. I don't know how he's going to react to my request. Particularly after I let him know I'm not requesting the full backing of the Bureau, or for them to get involved in the investigation again. This is all I need from him. Nothing more.

I knock on the door tentatively.

"Come in," his gruff voice comes. I enter to see him poring over files on his desk. After a second passes, he finally looks up at me.

"Griffin," he says with a mild note of surprise as if he hadn't actually seen who I was.

"Creagan, I need a favor."

"Is this another one of your personal cases?"

I take a deep breath. "Sort of?"

He rubs his temples and sets his jaw. "Griffin, how many times do we have to have this conversation? I can't use Bureau resources to look into your personal—"

"It's about my mother's murder," I interrupt him.

That gives him pause. I tell him the version of the story I'd rehearsed, doing my best to stick with exactly what will help him grant my request but not an inch more.

"You're sure about this?" he asks, stroking his chin.

"A hundred percent," I nod. "I'm confident whatever is in that casket will lead directly to the killers."

I'm not a hundred percent confident, but I don't have to tell him that.

He looks at me for a long moment, mulling it over in his head, then sighs.

"I'll put in the request first thing in the morning."

THE GIRL AND THE DEADLY END

I break into a grin. "Thank you so much, Creagan."

"Don't mention it. Now get out of here and do what you've gotta do before I change my mind."

I head back out into the snow, feeling like I'm moving forward. But there's a part of me that aches as I walk to the parking deck. Sam holds my hand tightly between us. He doesn't want to go back to my house any more than I do. We know when we do, he'll have to leave. There's still work to be done in Sherwood, and requesting the exhumation is creating even more work for him. Creagan will present the petition to the court, but having evidence of the break-ins at my house in Sherwood will make it more impactful. I can only hope the process is smooth and quick. I can't sit around and wait for approval.

We get to the house, and he leans across the car to rest his forehead against mine.

"Are you sure you're going to be alright?" he asks.

"I don't really have a choice," I tell him. "But I will. You do what needs to be done there, and I'll keep in touch with you."

"Please, do," he says. "I'm going to worry about you every second."

"I know you will. Thank you for that."

He laughs softly. "So now you're thanking me for worrying about you? That seems new."

"I guess I've grown," I tease.

Sam kisses me.

"Be safe," he says.

"I will have my phone and my gun with me at all times," I promise him.

"Keep your wits about you, too," he says. "That's usually the most important. I know you want this over. But when it is, I want you back home with me."

I want to promise him I will be, but I stop myself. With no idea of what's ahead of me or what I might be called on to do, I can't promise that. All I can do is kiss him again.

"I do, too," I whisper.

The lights aren't on inside the house, so Sam insists on checking everything before he goes. He says it's so I will feel safe being there alone, but I know it's just as much for his peace of mind. I wave goodbye to him with a knot in my throat. Not because I'm afraid, but because the uncertainty ahead makes me want him with me.

But this is the life I've chosen. I walked away from Sam once to pursue my career. I did it so I would never feel torn between what I needed to do for my career and the lifestyle I had at home. Now that I've gone back on that and made the decision to share my life with Sam again, I have to accept the balance. There will be times when duty will call both of us away. It just means we have to give everything we can while we're working, then make the most of every moment we can be together.

The house feels empty and quiet. When I turn on a light in my kitchen, I notice a piece of paper stuck to the front of the refrigerator with one of the random assortment of magnets Dad and I collected over the years. Seeing it puts me on edge. I grab hold of my phone as I approach it. My shoulders relax when I see Dean's name scrawled across the bottom.

"Won't be back tonight. See you tomorrow."

I immediately open my phone and call Bellamy. She stayed at headquarters after I left to help Eric, but she should be done by now. If I catch her fast enough, I might be able to rope her into an impromptu sleepover. The call is on its fourth ring when I hear a key in the front door.

"I'm sorry, I can't talk right now," Bellamy says into the phone as she walks in carrying a massive bag of Thai food.

"Too bad, I was going to ask you to come over," I say.

"Should have acted faster. I have a hot dinner date."

We end the call, and I cross the room to hug her.

"Thank you," I smile. "I don't think it would be a good idea for my brain to be alone tonight."

"I'm familiar with your brain," she replies. "Which is why I'm here. But it might be happy to know Creagan has already started the paperwork, and as soon as Sam gets him the information from the break-ins in Sherwood, they'll be able to submit the petition for the exhumation.

I let out a long, slow breath and nod as we walk into the living room. She starts unpacking the food, and I go into the bedroom to change into pajamas, then the bathroom to wash my face.

"Is it ridiculous I almost feel guilty about wanting to dig up her grave?" I ask as I sweep a warm cloth over my skin. "I didn't even know there was a grave, much less a casket to dig out of it. But it still feels strange to be sitting around, hoping a judge is going to give me permission to have a backhoe wrench her casket out of the ground."

"She would rather have you figure out what happened and put all this behind you than have a fake grave," Bellamy offers when I get back into the living room. "Not a sentiment I ever envisioned myself saying, but it stands."

As soon as the rich aromas of the food fill the living room and I have chopsticks between my fingers, we stop talking about everything looming over me. It's not gone from my mind. Nothing is going to take it out of my thoughts, but I can push it to the back of my mind and let it churn while I take some time away from it. We stay up talking late into the night, chasing away the darkness, and filling minutes I know will torment me otherwise. I'm in a holding pattern, and I hate it. I want to do something, to make progress, but for now, I wait.

Finally, I climb into bed, and seconds later drop into sleep.

CHAPTER TWENTY-THREE

Bellamy wakes me up to say goodbye before heading into work. Even with the heat on in the house, there's a distinct nip in the air. I'm tempted to roll over and create a cocoon with my blankets so I can just stay in bed for a few more hours. But I can't sleep. The second she wakes me up, my mind is jostled into full speed again, and after a few minutes of trying unsuccessfully to muffle it with my head stuffed under the pillow, I get up.

I make breakfast and catch up with Sam on the phone as I drink coffee and stare out the window at the thick layer of snow outside. I've never been a particularly big fan of snow in February. Not that it's not beautiful, but it always strikes me as out of place. By February, it seems we should be coming up on Spring, not still hiding under a frozen blanket. But there is something lovely about the morning sunlight sparkling on snow that hasn't yet been disturbed, and I choose to enjoy that about it. Sam and I talk for as long as he has time, then I bring my dishes into the kitchen and head for a shower. I'm not sure how long I stand in there, letting the hot water seep down into my bones like a protective layer to keep me warm for when I finally do face the outside. But when I get out, Dean is in the living room.

"You're back," I observe.

"I am," he replies, reaching for the coffee cup he has sitting on the table in front of him.

"Should I chalk up your ability to break into my house as one of your many illustrious private investigator skills?" I ask half-serious.

"No," he shrugs, continuing to scroll through something on his tablet without even looking at me. "You should chalk it up to Bellamy making me a copy of her extra key this morning."

"Perhaps not the most responsible thing to be out doing while I'm trying to avoid a serial killer," I point out.

This makes him lift his eyes to me.

"Do you think I have anything to do with it?" he asks.

"No," I tell him.

His eyes sink back to his tablet screen.

"Then you don't have anything to worry about," he says.

There are several fallacies in his thought process there, but I choose not to point them out. The truth is, I trust Dean. That was far from my mind when I first met him on the train, and again when I encountered him in Feathered Nest, but he's proven himself both reliable and valuable. And I can't overlook everything we have in common and the scars we both share. It's something other people can't understand, no matter how much they want to, and that makes me want to keep him close. I go into the kitchen and pour another cup of coffee from the fresh pot he brewed when he came in.

"Where were you last night?" I ask as I walk into the living room.

"In a hotel," he says. "There were some things I needed to get done, and I didn't want to be in your way or keep you up. I tend to get very little sleep when I'm invested in something."

I let out a short laugh and settle into the chair next to the couch, pulling my legs up, so I'm curled against the back with my cup cradled between my palms.

"That sounds so much like my father," I tell him. "I can remember when I was younger, my mom having to try to force him to sleep. He'd be up all night working on cases, and she would go into his office, take his glasses off and pull him out of the chair to bring him off to bed. Sometimes he would tell her he wanted a drink of water or forgot to turn the light off and sneak back in for another few minutes. She would tell him he was worse than a toddler."

Dean offers only the slightest hint of a smile. I'm about to ask him what he was working on last night when my phone alerts me to a message. It's an email from Eric with a subject line that just says 'test'.

My heart skips slightly. Sliding my legs down, so I'm sitting facing Dean, I open the message. An attachment shows the side-by-side comparison of our DNA profiles.

"The crime lab must have put a serious rush on our test," I say. "I just got the results."

"And?" He raises an eyebrow with anticipation.

I set my phone down and go for my tablet instead. The bigger screen will make it easier to see the attachment. Opening it, I turn the screen so both of us can see it. My eyes sweep over the explanation several times before I feel like it's really sunk in.

"The mitochondrial DNA is different, obviously, but we knew that. We have different mothers. But the other half shows similarities. That's exactly what I was expecting."

"What do you mean?"

"To somebody else reading these results, it would look like we're brother and sister. Like we have the same father. But we don't. We just happen to have fathers who share their DNA. Your father is my father's identical twin," I explain.

"We're cousins," he says.

I nod. "But Jonah is convinced he's father to both of us."

"Well," Dean says, setting his tablet down so I can see the screen. "He's apparently also dead."

I don't even know how to process what he just said. The words jumble up in my mind, and I can't force them into anything that makes sense.

"What are you talking about?" I ask. "Obviously, he's not dead."

"According to the government, he is. Jonah Griffin is legally dead. After you told us your theory yesterday, I couldn't get it out of my mind. I spent my entire life wondering who my father is, and what happened to him. Following you had nothing to do with that. I didn't know I was tracking down my family. It was really hard to wrap my head around it all, just trying to make sense of it. Suddenly I wasn't just finding out more about my mother and possibly getting an answer about her death; I was finding out about my father. And he's not exactly someone for me to be proud of."

"I'm sorry, Dean," I tell him.

He shakes his head.

"Don't be. It's a question I've always had, and if you hadn't found the answer for me, I would have just kept wondering. You got an answer for me. It might not be exactly the type of answer I thought I'd find, but it means I don't have to ask anymore. But, of course, I can't just let it go that easily. I'm a private investigator. Digging deeper is what I do. So last night, when I couldn't sleep, I started looking into Jonah Griffin, and I found this," he says, gesturing toward the tablet.

He shows me a scan of a death certificate.

"It says he died in 1998," I frown. "How is that possible? Could this belong to someone else with the same name?"

"No," Dean says. "It's him. All the other personal details are correct, and it's linked to the other information about him I was able to find."

"What other information?" I ask. "What were you able to find out about him?"

"He was born in Iowa, but you already knew that. He has an identical twin brother… "

"Knew that, too. All along I thought my father was an only child."

"From everything I found about him, his early life was normal. Jonah and Ian participated in activities together; they did well in school. But in college, Jonah started to show some potentially alarming leanings. He's got a rap sheet and was suspected of criminal activity, but they could never get a case on him. It looks like his relationship with Ian started to cool off quite a bit around then, but they were still spending time together and maintaining at least some connection immediately after college. Then things dropped off fairly dramatically about thirty years ago. I wasn't able to find anything else that linked the two of them."

"That's not surprising, considering that would be right around the time Jonah raped my mother. I'm sure by then, my father had picked up on his brother's obsession with his wife. That doesn't make for good family ties. I don't understand how you were able to find all this so quickly. I've looked into my father's life and done everything I could to understand his background, and I didn't find anything about his twin."

"I looked up Ian too, and it was almost like it was scrubbed. You just didn't know what to look for, so it was never there. But since Jonah was already dead, his records were left untouched. Somehow the two never made any official connection. That's why you couldn't find it."

"So, what happened after that? Where did he end up?" I ask.

"This is where it starts to get a little interesting. Department of Corrections records show Jonah Griffin serving time for a few years, but obviously, it had nothing to do with the rape. He was convicted of criminal trespass, stalking, and weapons charges."

"Who was he stalking?" I ask.

"The victim's name was redacted. After that, there's very little about him until the news of his death."

"What do they say happened to him?"

"Crushed and burned in a horrific car accident outside Sherwood, Virginia."

CHAPTER TWENTY-FOUR

"Police have presumptively identified the remains found in the wreckage of an auto accident late Wednesday night as belonging to Jonah L. Griffin, thirty-two. Sources confirm the chase leading to the accident followed an attempted crime, but police declined to provide details."

I scroll through the search results again and find another article, then another.

"They all say essentially the same thing," I say. "There was a chase that led to a horrific accident, the body was burned and mangled beyond recognition, but since Jonah was the only person to have been seen getting into that car and was known to be driving it prior to the crash, they identified the body as him."

"And issued him a death certificate," Dean adds.

"But whose death were they actually certifying?" I ask. "It doesn't just say that they assumed he was dead because of the damage to the vehicle. It specifically mentions remains. There was a body in that car."

"And he just let them assume it was him so he could slip away."

"Or that was his intention all along." I stare at the article again, and the date jumps out at me. "This article was written on August twenty-ninth. It says the accident was on Wednesday." I pull up a calendar and put in the year of the accident. "August twenty-sixth."

Dean's eyes get wide, and he moves closer to the edge of the cushion as if the realization is making it impossible for him to sit still.

"That's the day before your mother went to get the morning after pill," he says.

"The date he thought he and my mother conceived me, years before."

Just the thought makes my stomach turn. That's not a coincidence. Nothing this man does is by chance. He chose that day specifically, and the only reasoning that forms in my mind is sickening. I immediately dial Sam's number.

"Who are you calling?" Dean asks.

"Sam. He's the sheriff in Sherwood. He has access to the police records. Maybe he can tell us more about what happened that night."

"Miss me already?" Sam asks when he picks up the phone.

"No. I mean, yes, I do. But that's not why I'm calling," I say.

"That's reassuring."

"I'm sorry," I tell him. "I promise you I will miss you a lot when I have the chance. Right now, I need your help."

"What's going on?" he asks, his voice serious now.

"I need you to pull up a police report for me. August twenty-sixth, nineteen ninety-eight."

"What kind of police report? What happened?"

"Dean did some research into my uncle Jonah Griffin and found out he was issued a death certificate," I explain. "Supposedly he died in a car accident right outside Sherwood that night. Since we obviously know he didn't actually die, I want to know what really happened. All the news articles I've been able to find essentially talked about there being a chase that went on, and they found a body in the wreck. But obviously, that couldn't have been him. Apparently, he was involved in some sort of criminal activity that led to the crash, but the information was never released. I'm hoping it's in the police report."

"Absolutely, I'll do what I can," he replies. "Where are you going to be today?"

"Back at the hospital. I need to be there when Greg is awake so I can talk to him about everything. Hopefully, he'll be on less medication today. I need more info about Leviathan and what he was doing with Jonah. If he can tell us where he was kept, we might be able to find Jonah without incident."

Even as I say it, I know the chances of it actually working out that way are very slim. But I have to think that way. I have to balance my instincts with my training, hope for structure, and prepare for upheaval.

"I'll call you when I find the file," he says. "I know we already went over this, but please promise me you won't do anything impulsive. Or at least if you're going to, don't do it without someone knowing what's going on."

"If I have to do anything even remotely risky, I'll probably have my cousin with me."

It's the best way I can figure to slip the news into the conversation. Sam pauses.

"You got the results back."

"Yes. Jonah is Dean's father. Making him my cousin. He was so obsessed with my mother; he slept with the first woman who reminded him of her," I tell him.

"That's sick," he says. "We need to find this guy. That's not the kind of mind I want out on the streets."

"Then let's get him off them."

When the conversation is over, I call up to the hospital and check on Greg. Confirming he's awake and lucid, I finish getting ready, gather all the evidence I have of the bombing and Catch Me, and head for the hospital in the new rental car I had delivered this morning. My fingertips tingle with anticipation, waiting for my phone to ring so Sam can tell me what's in that file.

Greg's awake, looking a bit more lucid when I walk into his room. I've brought breakfast from the cafeteria, and his eyes light up.

"I don't know how your eating schedule is now, but I figured you might like a little bit of a break from the trays they bring you. So, I brought up a couple of sausage and egg biscuits, some hashbrowns, and some real coffee. How does that sound?" I ask.

"Sounds fantastic," he says.

"Good."

I set the food down on the tray table beside him, and Dean carries the files and bags of materials over to the sofa. Greg's eyes follow him.

"What's all that?" he asks.

I follow his gaze and let out a breath.

"I wanted to show you some things I uncovered while you were with Jonah and see if you could tell me anything about them," I say. He looks away, his eyes focusing on his feet at the end of the bed rather than me. "What's wrong?"

"You're talking about Lotan," he says, almost under his breath. "I've never heard his real name before."

"Yes," I tell him. He keeps staring, and I take a step closer to him. "Say it."

Greg looks over at me.

"What?"

"Say it," I repeat. "For two years, he forced you to call him by a title because he thinks he's a god. Let me tell you something. In ancient mythology, Lotan wasn't a god. He was a servant, a monster, and he was destroyed. You stood up to him. You survived him. Don't stay chained to him now."

"How do you know I stood up to him?" he asks.

"Because you're sitting here right now. You made sure your name was written in that book. And you tried to leave me something at the bus station when it was bombed. He might have had you in captivity, but you overcame it as much as you could."

Greg stares at me, and for the first time, I feel like we see each other. We're not hiding behind each other or trying to find something in the other that isn't there. For the first time, we're looking at each other and seeing the real person standing there.

"What do you have on Jonah?" he asks.

My lips curve into a hint of a smile, and I give a single nod before going over to the couch to gather what I brought with me. Greg takes a plate of breakfast into his lap and Dean takes another, sitting in the chair across the bed from me. I leave my plate on the tray table so I can take bites in between going through the papers and pictures spread across the bed and my lap.

"First, I want to know what you have. What is Leviathan?" I ask.

"I don't know exactly," he says.

"You were in it for two years," I point out incredulously.

"That's the thing. I was there, but I wasn't really in it. Not after the first few weeks, anyway. Jonah is cruel and deluded, but he's brilliant. He has tight control over everyone around him. Nobody knows all the details except for him. Even the highest-ranking members are still kept in the dark about some things. There is a very strict hierarchy in the organization. You learn more as you move up. I was brought in higher in the rankings than the disposable pawns he uses essentially for filler, but I didn't stay in his good favor long enough to gain his trust and learn more. What I do know is his philosophy. Jonah believes in the power of chaos. He thinks the world is sleeping. That most people never actually live. Chaos, fear, and destruction give energy and value to life, and promote power and influence."

"Chaos. Tiamat," Dean pipes up. "Remember? When we were trying to figure out what Martin was talking about when he was rambling about Lotan, we read about the Mesopotamian goddess that represented the chaos of creation."

"There is also the tradition that Leviathan is the representation of destruction," Greg says. "In Christianity, Leviathan is often used for the imagery of Satan and his destruction of everything. But he's also referred to as the demon of envy."

My eyes go to Dean.

"Can you think of anyone Jonah might have been envious of?" I ask.

Dean nods, the same link forming in his mind.

"Just like Leviathan means different things, it has different forms," Greg continues. "Every member is devoted to the concept of chaos and power, but those are often different things. Jonah selects his followers carefully. Uses them for everything they have to offer. Some aid his pursuit of wealth, influence, or control with trafficking. I personally was involved with dealings with the drug cartels and weapons sales."

"What about the others?" I ask.

"Some agents instigate chaos directly. Terrorist attacks. Staged destructions. Mass shootings. He plans the destruction, and they ensure it happens," Greg tells me.

"Was he involved in the bombing of the bus station?" I ask. I reach down and pull out the files I have from the investigation. "I didn't think you had anything to do with it."

Greg shakes his head.

"I didn't. That wasn't the plan. Jonah was furious when that happened. He sent hunters out to find the person responsible, but no one has been able to find them."

"Why was he so angry?" Dean asks. "If he loves chaos so much, why would he be upset about something that destructive?"

"Because he didn't control it. It wasn't designed around his plan. And he was afraid for you, Emma. You're the focus of everything."

"What?" I gasp.

"Everything he does. Every attack, every plan, every destruction, he does it with you in mind."

That makes my skin crawl. I push it aside, focusing on the question I've carried with me since I saw the footage of him.

"What did you give to the man at the information desk?" I ask. "The FBI has footage of you going into the station right before the blast." I show him a still from the video. "You have a bag, and you put it in the locker. Then you go to the information desk. I know you gave them something for me."

Greg nods.

"I wasn't bringing something to the station. I was facilitating a pickup. One of Jonah's connections left a payment for a shipment of guns in one of the lockers. It was my job to go to that locker, put the payment in the bag, then put that bag in a different locker. The plan was for it to be moved again later before finally being picked up.

That's the way he did everything, making sure he didn't leave any straight lines to follow."

"But you did leave something at the desk," I say.

"I hoped someone would notice something. That there would be an investigation and the Bureau would be brought in. I tried to leave as many clues in as many places as I could. I knew you weren't going to find all of them, but if you could find any of them, it would tell you I was alive and hopefully eventually lead you to him. It wanted to leave things you would know instantly were for you and from me, but that wouldn't give too much away, so it didn't create more danger."

"What was that one?"

"A note saying I would be at the restaurant at nine," he says.

We both let out soft, sad laughs.

"That would have done it," I tell him.

CHAPTER TWENTY-FIVE

"Where were you?" Dean asks. "Where did they keep you?"

"I don't know," Greg says. "Not exactly, anyway. Lotan—Jonah—made sure we never went the same route twice to the compound. It was another secret he kept from most members. At first, he had me convinced it was to protect the confidentiality of the undercover assignment. He told me the fewer details I knew at the beginning, the better. I would learn more as the job progressed. But once he realized I knew he wasn't Ian and that something else was going on, it just became a matter of control."

"But it was close?" I ask. "Around here somewhere?"

"It took probably an hour to get to where we stayed most of the time, but we rarely were in one place for long. He had us traveling all over."

"How?" I ask. "How did you travel?"

"Jonah has a tremendous amount of influence. His network is huge. If it wasn't for the sheer evil it's allowed for; I'd say it was impressive. There was always a car or plane ready to take us wherever we needed to go. No documentation needed. Wherever we went, we stayed in houses, never hotels. They were always people ready to welcome him and do whatever he needed," Greg explains.

"Alright. What can you tell us about his most trusted people? You said you were not his most trusted, but you were above others."

"Yes," he nods. "I was one of the 'honored', as he likes to describe it. I was brought in to listen to his rants about you and the life he was creating for you. In the beginning, he almost treated me like a friend, but really, he was trying to glean as much information from me as he possibly could. When he realized I wasn't fully under his spell, he just tried to torture it out of me."

"I'm so sorry," I tell him.

"Don't be. None of this is your fault. You couldn't possibly have known what was happening. Besides, I thought I was getting involved in a critical undercover assignment that would bring down pervasive organized crime and terrorism. Maybe after everything I went through in there, that's actually what I'm getting to do now."

I nod.

"We're going to find him. And we're going to stop him."

"I know you are," he says.

"Does the name Martin Phillips mean anything to you?" Dean asks. "Did you know him when you were in there?"

"Martin?" Greg asks.

"He's an orderly here at the hospital," I explain. "Or at least, he was. He's been taking care of you since you came in, but a couple of days ago, he drugged me and stuffed me in a body drawer in the morgue. Dean rescued me, and we realized Martin was missing. No one has seen him since, and the police investigation has come up with nothing. The only thing we were able to uncover is a video diary he made. He posted several videos on a private blog ranting completely incoherently about Lotan. That's how we heard the name, to begin with. Did you know him?"

"None of us knew anybody by our actual names," he says. "Just like Lotan, we were all called something different."

"Did you get to decide what you were called?" I ask.

"No. Lotan chose it for us."

"Of course he did," Dean says.

The disgust in Dean's voice is more pronounced now. Finding out his true paternity is crawling under his skin and digging into his soul. It's chipping away at him, and I can only hope bringing an end to this will give him the vindication he needs.

I want to ask the question that's on the very tip of my tongue, to find out what Jonah called Greg when he was under his power. But I stop myself. After everything he went through, the last thing Greg needs is to ever hear that name again. Whatever it was, it needs to stay wherever he pushed it until he wants to say it. Instead, I ask around it.

"What kind of names?"

"All kinds of things. It depends on the person and what they did within Leviathan. The ones closest to him were given new names. The man who signed the guest book was called Finn. He is the only person I know of other than me to get out alive. The only reason he had the opportunity was because he got close to Lotan. He was able to feed me more information about what was going on, and when he left, he offered to bring me."

"Why didn't you go?"

"You were in danger. You still are. I needed to do everything I could to keep you safe," he says. Something close to humor sparkles in his eyes briefly. "I'm not vying for your heart, Emma. It wasn't chivalry. You will always matter to me, but our past is our past."

I nod my acknowledgement, not trusting myself to say anything about it. The guilt that started fading when the veil lifted between us loosens further, and it's like I've been released.

"Can you think of any other names?" I ask.

"There was one. He was involved in several of the bigger plans while I was there and spent a lot of time with Lotan. He was very loyal and very devoted to continuing the mission. He had a gift for finding people to use as bait for Lotan's schemes. I guess that's how he got his name. Jonah called him Fisher."

I take my laptop out and click on the window I already have up. Martin's blog appears, and I show Greg, not starting the video.

"This is Martin. Does he look familiar?"

Greg looks at it for a few seconds, slowly shaking his head.

"I don't think so. Can I watch it?" he asks.

"Are you sure you want to?"

"I want to hear what he has to say."

I start the video. My eyes flicker back and forth to him, gauging his expression as he watches. It's steady, almost cold, but I know it has to be affecting him. At the end of the video, he shakes his head again.

"No. I don't know him. But that doesn't mean much. Much of the control involved keeping us apart or against each other. You didn't cross Lotan. The biggest risk I took wasn't leaving that note for you or even resisting Jonah. It was deciding to trust Finn. He could have been a spy. He could have turned me in to Jonah, and that would have been far worse than anything I faced."

"Okay," I nod, feeling some of the hope and optimism I had draining away.

"What is it?" Greg asks. "What is it about him? I know it's more than just him mentioning Leviathan."

Dean and I exchange glances. Greg already said he didn't know Martin and wasn't familiar with anyone else in the organization. The thought of putting even more stress and trauma onto him by telling him about Catch Me makes me hesitant, but at the same time, he might know more than he realizes. Even the smallest detail could be valuable now.

"Jonah isn't the only person putting me in danger," I tell him.

"What do you mean?"

Tucking away the papers I already took out, I bring out everything I have about Catch Me and start to unravel it all. He listens in silence, evaluating every picture and occasionally nodding as he tries to take it all in. I've gotten to the note supposedly from Marren Purcell that brought me to the train when my phone rings. Seeing it's Sam, I look at Dean.

"I've got it," he says.

I realize he does. I've gotten to the strange point in the story where we thought our lives overlapped, not realizing we were linked from long before. Leaving Dean to tell Greg more, I take my phone out and head for the lounge.

"Hey," I say, answering the phone. "I miss you. I figured I should get that over with at the beginning of the conversation."

"I appreciate it," Sam says. "I miss you, too. But I have a feeling I'll be seeing you soon."

"What do you mean?" I ask. "Are you already coming back?"

"No, but I think you might want to come home."

"Sam, I can't. I'm right in the middle of all of this. Greg is giving us more details and what he doesn't know we're trying to piece together. I can't leave it alone now," I tell him as I reach for the bag of coffee to start a new pot.

"No, you can't. Which is why you need to be here to see these reports," he says.

"Reports? I thought there was only one about the wreck."

"There was. But there are others about what led up to it. You really need to see them, Emma. It has to do with your parents. And with you."

Fresh coffee sizzles and spits on the hot plate as I snatch the partially filled pot away and tip it into a cup. Snapping a lid on it, I rush back toward Greg's room.

"I'm on my way."

CHAPTER TWENTY-SIX

MARIYA

TWENTY-TWO YEARS AGO...

Mariya lifted her mouth from the edge of her teacup to call out to her young daughter as she ran through the house toward the front door.

"Emma, darling, put on a sweater before you go out. It's chilly."

"No, it's not," Emma said. "It's sunny out there."

The young mother laughed.

"We aren't in Florida, my love. Here Autumn is when the world starts to go to sleep for the year. Remember when we came for Thanksgiving? That is only two and a half months away," she said.

Curious and determined, Emma stared back at her, stuck between believing her mother and already finding her own way in the world. That was one of the many things Mariya loved about her. She was strong and believed first in what she knew within herself, above what she was told. Mariya hoped she would hang on to that as she got older. It's more difficult as an adult to find the balance. To believe wholly in yourself and also be willing to trust.

"Two and a half months is a long time, Mama," Emma said.

"You're right. Find out for yourself. Step outside, and you'll see," Mariya shrugged.

Holding her ball beneath her arm, Emma stepped out onto the front porch. She stood there for a few moments before backing into the house and closing it. Setting the ball down, she rushed to her room and came back seconds later, shrugging into her favorite bright yellow sweater. Mariya brought her mouth back to her teacup to muffle her laughter.

"Can I go?" Emma asked. "Dad is out there."

"Can he see you?" she asked.

"Yes," Emma nodded. "He's just in the side yard fixing the fence. He'll be able to see me."

"Alright, then. But don't go anywhere he can't see you."

"I won't."

Mariya waited a few seconds before getting up from the dining room table and crossing the living room to the large front window. She didn't want her daughter to know she was watching her. As hard as it was for her, she was trying to encourage independence in Emma. She was only seven years old. There wasn't much she could do completely on her own, but Ian and Mariya wanted her to feel confident and able to make decisions for herself. They loved her and trusted her, but they were so afraid for her. If anyone understood the risks and dangers lurking in the world, it was the two of them. They had seen the worst in people. They witnessed the cruelty and viciousness of life and knew just how quickly a safe, normal life could fall into treacherous waters.

Their instinct was to protect her. They wanted to shield her from everything. But they knew that would only limit her. It was far more important to help her take her place in the world. To slowly prepare her for what she might one day experience.

Mariya knew this and tried to follow it every day. But it didn't stop her from always wanting to guard her daughter. She stood there by the window, not just keeping an eye on Emma. It was really about savoring every moment she had with her. She was growing up so fast.

It seemed like Emma should still be just a baby, cradled in her arms. The days had gone by so fast. They disappeared in an instant and left her reaching for them, trying to hang on as much as she could.

The last week had been difficult on Mariya. It was the first time in a few months she'd been away from Emma for more than just a weekend. But she had to do as much as she could in those days to prepare them for coming here. They were planning on spending the next few months, at least through the end of the year, in Sherwood. Mariya would travel as necessary to help women in the area as much as possible, but she would stay close to the family. Those were the days she never liked to face. Days she often stared at on the calendar, dreading their arrival. She would celebrate when they were finally behind her.

She coped with it in silence. Not that she didn't think Ian knew. He watched her go through the anxiety and pain every year. Neither of them liked to talk about it. This year they decided they wouldn't. They would move past it by going to spend time with his parents and enjoying a calmer pace for a little while.

Emma settled down immediately. She always did. She was adaptable. Willing to go with the ever-changing life they led as long as they were together. Mariya knew she hated when either of her parents left home. But it was easier for her when Ian was gone. The little girl missed her father desperately, but as long as Mariya stayed steady and let her know everything was all right, Emma felt calm. It wasn't as easy when she needed to be gone. Mariya knew it was because Emma didn't understand why she left. She knew about her father's job, at least in the way such a little girl could know. But they hadn't told her about what her mother did.

Emma didn't know about the women or the other small children that they rescued. She didn't know that when Mariya left it was with a weapon on her hip and a prayer in her soul that she'd be able to deliver those families out of suffering and into new lives. She never let herself dwell on the reality that she might not come home to her own life.

She'd entertained a thought about stopping. For a time. Many

A.J. RIVERS

years ago. Just after Emma came into the world, she held her tiny newborn daughter in her arms and looked into her face, thinking about how precious and delicate she was. Mariya wondered how she could ever leave her, how she could ever go back out into that danger and risk her daughter not having her anymore.

Then she remembered those who relied on her. Many of them had children, and those who didn't might someday. Those mothers would look into their babies' faces the same way she looked into Emma's. They didn't deserve to fear what would happen to them.

That's what sent her back out. It's what made her push harder and believe deeper. One day she would tell Emma about all of it. She would explain to her what she did and show her the records she kept. Those were valuable to her. The names and the faces, the real people who gave her purpose. Her belief would sometimes falter. Some missions didn't go as planned. Sometimes the women fell victim despite her best efforts. Each one like a wrench tearing apart her soul. But she could always go to those records, scan through them, remembering those who were able to walk out of the darkness and claim their own piece of light.

But for now, Emma was just an innocent little girl. She didn't want her to know about the horrors of the world. For now, Mariya was happy to just watch her play.

Outside the window, Emma bounced her ball on the sidewalk and occasionally ran across the grass to talk to her father. After a few seconds, the ball slipped from her hands and started rolling toward the street. Worry jumped in Mariya's heart, and she made a move to go to the front door, ready to call Emma back from running out into the street. But she didn't need to. A little boy maybe a couple of years older than Emma was riding his bike past the house and stopped just before hitting the ball. He got off his bike and grabbed the ball to bring it back over to Emma. They looked at each other for a brief moment as he carefully placed the ball in her hands.

It was a sweet moment, so tender and innocent. She only turned away when the phone rang. Jogging into the kitchen, she picked the phone up from the cradle.

"Hello?" she answered, expecting to hear her mother-in-law's voice on the other end.

Ian's parents weren't there when they arrived the night before but were supposed to return that night. She expected the call to be from them to make plans for dinner or to say they would be home earlier than expected. Instead, Elliot's voice came through sharp and urgent. He was supposed to be in Texas, escorting a woman they just took from a truly unimaginable situation in Michigan. Getting a call from him meant something was wrong. He didn't get in touch with her like this, especially not on this number. It created too much of a trail, too much of something to follow and link back between the women and her.

"Get inside and lock the doors."

"I am inside. That's how I answered the phone," Mariya pointed out. "What's going on?"

"Is Emma with you? And Ian?"

"She's outside playing in the yard, and he's with her. Elliot, what is happening?"

She rarely spoke his real name if they weren't in the same room. It was too risky. But right now, she wasn't thinking of anything but the urgency in his voice.

"Get them inside. Lock the doors. I'm at the airport right now. I'm getting the next plane out."

"You need to tell me what's happening right now," she commanded.

"He's there."

"What?"

"Jonah."

Her stomach fell, and her hand gripped the phone harder.

"He's there, Mariya. In Sherwood. Or at the very least he's on his way. Doc has been tracing him and found out he tracked your movements and headed for you."

"When?"

It was all she could manage.

"Earlier today. Don't try to leave the area. You don't want him following you and separating you from them. Get in the house, hunker down, and wait for me. I transferred Leah to Paul in Atlanta. He'll get her to Texas, and I'm on my way to Virginia. I'll get there as fast as I can. If you see him, call the police."

CHAPTER TWENTY-SEVEN

NOW

"I can't believe I didn't put it together when you first started talking about it," Sam says. We're in the evidence room of the Sherriff's Office in Sherwood poring over the files. "But I remember that night. It was chilly that day, but not too cold. I went out to ride my bike. I was going through the different neighborhoods, and I saw a girl playing with a ball in the front yard."

"Me," I nod. "I remember that now. I was playing, and I lost control of the ball. You were riding your bike, and I thought you were going to hit it. I was worried you were going to fall. But you stopped and picked it up and brought it to me."

"I rode around for a little bit longer and then headed home for dinner. But I wasn't there very long when my dad got a call. He told my mom there was a disturbance at the Griffin house. He had to be talking about your grandparents. She asked him if everything was all right. He kind of shrugged her off like he didn't know what was going on, but he was gone for the rest of the night. The next day when he got home, they talked about the accident. I didn't know what happened, but later on the news, I saw the story about the crash and that somebody died. Dad was really shaken up about it. It really got to him. I had no idea the two things had anything to do with each other. They wouldn't talk about it in front of me," he tells me.

Looking at the reports and evidence boxes spread out on the table in front of me is like looking at a brutal scrapbook. Vaults locked tight in the back of my mind crack open. Memories I never wanted to experience again seep out into my consciousness.

"My mother came outside and grabbed me. It scared me at first; then I thought she might be playing. I tried to wriggle away from her so we could play tag, but she held me tight and ran for the house, shouting for my father. I dropped my ball. I remember being so worried about it. It was rolling down the sidewalk again, and I didn't want it to get away. I tried to get out of her arms again, and she told me to stop. She yelled at me. It was the first time in my life I can remember her really raising her voice at me. She sounded so angry, and I didn't know what I had done. Dad went and got my ball, and we went inside. He locked all the doors, and she put me down but told me I had to stay right there and not to move. She ran around the house, pulling all the blinds down and checking the windows. It was like a bad storm was coming."

"It was," Sam says. "Just not like you might have thought. The first call my father took to the house was when they noticed Jonah outside. There really wasn't anything he could do about it, though, because he didn't get near the house, and technically he had the right to visit his parents just as much as Ian did. The notes in here say the brothers had been estranged for several years, and that tension made it so Ian didn't want Jonah around."

"Of course they were estranged," I note. "After what he did, my father wouldn't want anything to do with Jonah."

"Well, Jonah clearly didn't get the message because before my father could even get home, he had broken into the house, and your father was chasing him. That must have been the criminal activity the newspapers didn't want to report on," Sam says. "Since Jonah died in the wreck, they couldn't speculate on what he was doing at the house."

"Doesn't need any speculation," I say. "The day he came to the house was the anniversary of the day he raped my mother. He was there because he believed it was the anniversary of the day he conceived his child with my mother. This the first time he's tried to come for me. Jonah was there that night to claim me back."

"But your father chased him away, and it started raining. There really was a storm coming. I remember that now. There was a horrible thunderstorm that night that started just after my father left the house. It would have gotten to its worst when they were driving. Your father must have got in his car and was chasing his brother before the storm made Jonah lose control. He crashed into the ravine off the side of the back road."

"No, Sam. It wasn't an accident. Look at the accident report. There's no evidence here of a second car skidding on the road. My father might have gone after him, but he wasn't chasing him when the car went off the road. The articles talk about a chase earlier, not that the car was involved in the wreck. And they never mention my father because there were no criminal charges. Jonah planned that. He planned, if he couldn't get his hands on me, what he was going to do next. That body was already in the car," I point out.

"Why would he do that? What was the point of faking his own death?" Sam asks.

"Because nobody hides from a dead man," I say. My eyes go wide. A memory snaps like a bolt of lightning behind my eyes, nearly making my knees buckle. "We need to go to my house."

"Right now?" he asks.

"Yes. We need to go now," I tell him.

As soon as Sam's squad car pulls up in front of my house, I tumble out and run around the back of the house. Going into the small shed, I grab the axe my father used to use for firewood off the wall and run inside.

"What are you doing with that?" Sam asks.

"There's a reason Jonah left here without me," I say as I make my way through the house toward the attic stairs. "You talked about the storm that night. I love storms. I love to sit by the window and watch them. Always have."

"I know you do," he says.

"I didn't watch that one. I remember hearing it, but I couldn't see it. There was nowhere to look out and see the rain."

"How is that?" he asks. "Every room in this house has windows."

"Not every room," I say and sprint up to the attic.

The lightbulb glows yellow down on the wooden floor. Shadows are moving on the wall from the boxes and furniture that have gradually filled the space. I find the spot on the wall where a hulking armoire used to sit. My hands grip the handle of the axe, rage creeping up my body and flowing into my hands. Rage at my uncle for what he did to my mother. Rage at my mother's death and never seeing her face again. Rage at being followed and watched. Rage at Catch Me.

Rage at myself for allowing myself to be played like this.

But no more.

I let out a cry and swing it hard. The blade bites into the wall. I yank it back with every bit of strength I can gather and slam it again into the attic wall.

"Emma, what are you doing?" Sam demands, scrambling up the steps into the attic. "Put the axe down."

"No!" I snap. "Enough secrets! Enough hiding. Enough of all of it. Pam told us there was a room up here."

I wrench the blade out again, sending drywall and chips of the wallpaper scattering, and swirling dust into my eyes and mouth. I cover my cough and swing again, digging deeper. "I said there wasn't. That I remember this place from when I was a little girl. I would remember a room."

Another swing causes a large section of the wallpaper to come down and the wall to crack and break apart. One more reveals a door.

"Holy shit," Sam gasps behind me. "Not a room that was hidden."

"I couldn't see the storm that night because Mama brought me up here. We hid in this room. I didn't remember it from when I was younger because there wasn't anything to remember about it. And then I blocked out that night. I blocked out being terrified because I knew somebody was trying to get into the house and hurt us. I was terrified when Dad ran out of the house after him. I didn't know who it was. They never told me about Jonah. For obvious reasons now. Dad came home, and I heard the police come back. He said something about not seeing anything. He just heard the crash. I had no idea what he was talking about. Mama kept me in the bedroom after we came down from here. My grandparents showed up, and I spent the rest of the evening with my grandmother. I had no idea what happened. Only that there was a lot of crying that night," I told him. "A big armoire used to sit against this wall. I always thought it was there to store my grandma's old coats, not to hide something. That's how I knew where to look. They must have boarded it up sometime after that night."

"But why would they board up this room?" Sam asks. "What would be the point in sealing it up? They believed your uncle was dead, but that doesn't mean they have to get rid of the hiding spot. Especially considering every other house on this street has this extra room. It's not like it would stand out."

I look at the door and the bits of wall surrounding it. Touching my fingertips to the drywall and plaster used to seal up the room, I realize sections of it are a different color than the rest.

"The room was sealed up twice," I point out. "Look. Some of this is older than others. Somebody went into the room after it was already closed up."

"Let's find out what they were after," he says, taking the axe from my hand.

I step back while Sam chips away at the rest of the wall to reveal the door completely. He sets the axe down, and I step up to the door, resting my hand on the knob. I have no idea what to expect on the other side. My heart shakes in my chest. My mind screams at me to just seal it back up and walk away. They sealed the room for a reason, and I shouldn't disturb it. But I can't. I've lived my entire life with gaps in my past. Black stretches where I should have days. Question marks where I should have memories. My mother's death and my father's disappearance made me feel like I would never fill those spaces. Now I have the chance to. I can't turn my back on it. Whatever is inside is another piece toward understanding it all.

CHAPTER TWENTY-EIGHT

"It's like they took his entire life and shoved it in here," I muse. "They literally sealed him up. Made him disappear."

Sam and I have stepped into the small room off the attic. We're staring at shelves and boxes of... memorabilia, for lack of a better word. Not for a sports team or a treasured alma mater. But for a life. The room overflows with pictures, trophies, and clothing. Childhood trinkets are piled alongside photographs. There's even a pair of boots leaned in the corner like they're waiting to be put on.

"It looks like they took everything that belonged to him and put it in here," Sam agrees.

"And everything my grandparents had of him," I point out. "These look like pictures that would have been hanging on the wall and pages of albums. They took all of the reminders that Jonah existed and put them in here, then sealed it up and walked away like he never existed."

"But why would they keep it?" Sam asks. "They thought he was dead. After everything he did, I can understand not wanting to think about him. I can even understand them not wanting you to know he ever existed. Not knowing what he did to your mother, and that he tried to come after you. Maybe even more than once. They would want to protect you by not letting you know. But if it was that important to them, if they really wanted to obliterate him from history, why keep a room full of reminders of him? It's almost like a shrine."

"It's not a shrine," I reply. "Everything was just put in here. It's not on display. No one was ever able to access it."

"I still don't understand," he says. "Why keep it at all?"

"Because he was their child," I say. "Sam, this wasn't my mother and father's house. This was my grandparents' house. They knew what he did and understood why he needed to be removed from their family's lives, but that didn't change that they had two sons. My grandmother carried two babies inside her. She gave birth to two boys. She raised them and loved them. She watched them become men. A mother doesn't just stop loving her child even if she has to excise him from her daily life. He was still her son."

"Are you seriously sympathizing with him?"

"No. I'm sympathizing with parents who had to live with knowing one son betrayed the other so badly. Who had to mourn his death in silence. They believed he was dead. They marked the end of his life by pretending it never happened. And don't forget, he and my father are identical twins. So, every time they looked at my father's face, they saw Jonah, too."

On the other side of the room, I notice a plain white box that looks like boxes my dad used to store stuff. I take off the top, using my phone light to look inside. It's filled with file folders. Sam comes up beside me as I take one out and open it.

"What are those?" he asks.

"I think they're the reason somebody unsealed the sealed room," I tell him. He glances over my shoulder, and I show him the file. "This is my father's handwriting." He takes the folder from me, and I grab out another few. "These all have my father's handwriting in them. These are his records."

"Why would he put them in here?" Sam asks.

"Look at the dates. These cover years. Most of them are from before the wreck. But then, look, he didn't write the date on these."

I pull a newspaper clipping out of the box. "It's from six months before he disappeared." I open another of the folders, and a vice tightens around my heart. "Sam..."

He looks up from the file he's holding, and I show him the picture in my hand.

"That's Natalia," he says.

I nod. "This whole file is about her death."

"It seems your father was doing a lot of looking into your future," he tells me.

"What do you mean?" I ask. He shows me the folder in his hands so I can read it. Across the top of the page, in my father's handwriting, is a phrase: *"What is he doing?"* I read out loud. "He knew about Leviathan."

"At least he had his suspicions," Sam nods. "There's nothing in here that's specific. It doesn't directly talk about Leviathan or refer to Jonah as Lotan. But there are notes about accidents and disasters he believes were actually crimes. It seems he figured out Jonah wasn't dead."

"But why would he take all this and put it in here? Why would he go to the effort of opening up a sealed room to hide files in it?" I ask.

"He didn't want anyone else to find them?" Sam suggests. "He knew there could be danger and didn't want anyone else to get their hands on this information, but also couldn't just destroy it."

"Derrick mentioned my father came here just a little while before he disappeared. He said he was clearing some stuff out of the house and putting it in the storage so the house could be rented. We've gone to the storage unit, so we know he actually did that. But what if he wasn't just putting stuff into the storage unit. What if he was hiding these, too?"

"Because he knew he wouldn't be looking at them any time soon," Sam says. "Either he knew he would be back for them, or that one day you would find them. By this point, he knew Jonah was alive. This room wasn't about pretending his brother never existed anymore. One day it was all going to come out. He just had to keep it safe until then."

"This would explain what he was looking for when he broke into the house. He just didn't have time to find it," I say. I put the files back into the box and put the lid on before lifting it and heading out of the room. "I want to go through these more carefully. Maybe Dad was onto something that can help us."

My phone starts ringing in my pocket when I'm halfway down the attic stairs. I let it ring as I lug the box into the living room. By the time I've set the box down on the living room table, the ringing stops. I take out my phone and look at the screen.

"Who was it?" Sam asks.

"It was Dean," I frown, concern immediately building in my chest. "He stayed at the hospital with Greg to try to get as much information as he could. Hope everything's okay."

Sam opens the box and starts taking the files out as I redial Dean's number.

"Hey," I say when he answers. "I'm sorry I missed your call. Is everything okay?"

"Martin put up a new video," he tells me with no introduction.

"A new video?" I ask.

"Greg wanted to watch the videos again to see if he could pull out any information he missed the first time. When I opened the blog again, there was a new video posted. You might want to check it out."

"Hold on; I'll watch it right now. I just need to grab my computer."

Sam and I sit side-by-side on the couch as I access the blog. Just like Dean said, a new video was posted just a couple of hours ago. Holding my phone to my ear with one hand, I use the other to start the video. Unlike in the other videos, Martin is outside. Wind whips around him as he walks.

"All will come to pass soon. Lotan knows I have failed him. I did all I could. But I will make atonement. I will make it right."

The video jostles and then drops as if the camera fell or Martin put it down on the ground and then goes silent.

"What happened? I can't hear anything," I say.

"The audio got turned off," Dean explains.

"On purpose?"

"I don't think so. I think the intention was to turn the camera off. Keep watching," he tells me.

There's not much to see. The camera angle shows the ground at the bottom edge of the screen and the sky at the top. The side goes dark for a few moments, like Martin stepped in front of it, then brightened again. A few seconds later, something drops in front of the camera. At first, it doesn't register what I'm looking at. Then it sinks in.

"That's the blade of a scalpel," I say.

"And it's bloody," Sam adds.

The camera moves again, and for just a second, the audio comes back, then the screen goes dark, and the video ends.

"We need to find him," I say.

"How?" Dean asks. "He doesn't say where he is."

"Hold on," I say. I scan back a few seconds and watch the end of the video again. It takes two more times going through it before I'm sure. "I know where he is."

CHAPTER TWENTY-NINE

"Care to explain to me how you knew there was a body here?"

"Lovely to speak to you again, too, Detective Legends," I say.

The screen of the video call is fairly dark, but there's just enough illumination for me to see the scowl on the angry detective's face.

"I'm not in the mood for your bullshit, Miss Griffin," he says through gritted teeth.

"Agent Griffin," I correct him. Again.

He somehow contorts his face even further and continues. "The last I heard from you and Sheriff Johnson, the two of you were leavin' in the middle of our investigation. Then on the news, I saw you got yourself tangled up in another murder in Feathered Nest. I thought you were their problem, but now I get dragged away from my night off 'cause of a tip about someone in trouble. And lo and behold, who is behind that call, but you? So, I wanna know again. How did you know there was going to be a body here?"

"I already explained it to the officers I spoke to," I fire back.

"My jurisdiction, my case. So, explain it to me," he snaps.

"Is that Emma?" I hear a much more pleasant voice ask from off-camera.

"Yes," Legends growls. The screen shifts. Detective Mayfield's face appears on my phone.

"Hi, Emma," he smiles.

"Hi," I nod. "I see you're still yoked to the delightful Detective Legends. Haven't figured out how to get out of that yet?"

The younger detective opts to remain diplomatic and doesn't feed into my negativity toward his partner, opting instead to mutter a small laugh and smile.

"Can you tell me what's going on?" he asks. "We just got your tip that we'd find somebody out here who needed help."

He doesn't need help. There's nothing anyone can do for Martin now. The hospital sheet around his slashed neck assured that. But someone needed to find him sooner than the hours it would take to drive down there.

I give Detective Mayfield a brief recounting of the events. When I finish, he stares back at me with widened eyes that don't seem to belong to a man who's handled many murders in his career. But that's what makes him good at what he does. Even after everything he's seen and all the evil he's witnessed, Mayfield still manages to have feelings and sympathy. It's what keeps him caring and stops him from getting complacent.

"Well, at first glance, it looks like Martin was feeling guilty about failing the leader of his cult and killed himself to make up for it," he says.

"Martin didn't kill himself," I say.

"And you know that so clearly why?" Detective Legends demands, snatching the phone back from his younger partner.

"It doesn't fit," I offer.

"Evidently, you didn't watch the video close enough," he says. "Martin here said he was gonna atone for what he did. For his failures."

"Killing himself wouldn't be an atonement," I point out. "That wouldn't do any good. The man he was referring to, Lotan, doesn't care if his followers live or die. It would mean nothing to him to have someone kill themselves because of him. I wouldn't put it past him to have a collection. But that's not the point. The point is, I did watch the video close enough to notice the bits of sand splash up against the lens of the camera when the scalpel dropped. And in the last couple seconds of audio that came back on, I heard the train whistle."

"And you honestly want me to believe that was enough for you to figure out he was at the train station?" Legends growls.

"Detective, you're getting dangerously close to accusing me of murder again," I say, forcing my voice to remain as calm as possible.

"If the scalpel fits," he says sarcastically.

"I really don't want to have to remind you that a man is dead, not three feet away from you," I say. "Try to show a little bit of professionalism and respect."

"Don't tell me how to do my job," Legends growls. "If you would stop getting in the way of everything, it would be better for everybody."

"I'm several hundred miles away from you," I point out. "If that makes me in your way, you seriously need to reevaluate your sense of personal space."

The phone goes back into Detective Mayfield's hand.

"How did you figure out it was the train station?" he asks. "Those details are suggestive, but not enough to narrow in on a place like this."

"I didn't need to have it narrowed. This killer is tracking me. Everything he does is about me and what I'm doing. He already chose that place. When the train stopped there, the spot was chosen. It's possible he didn't have a plan at the time, but when he chose Martin as the next set of clues, that place came to mind because he's familiar with it, and he knew I would be, too."

"And you're confident he was murdered?" Mayfield asks.

"People don't slit their own throats and then hang themselves, Detective."

"That isn't the only injury, Detective," another voice says.

"Who's that?" I asked.

"Andy Gallmeyer, ma'am," a very young-looking man says as

Mayfield turns the phone toward him. "I'm on the team evaluating the scene."

"You said there are other injuries? I only got a very brief glimpse of Martin's hanging corpse, not enough to give me any real insight into anything other than the gash on his throat."

"His back is a bloody mess," Andy says. 'It looks like it's been flayed. An entire section of the skin is missing."

"Can you explain that, Griffin?" Legends asks.

"Are you asking for my help, Legends?" I ask. "A feeble attempt at humility isn't a good look on you."

"I'm far from asking for your help," the detective grumbles. "At this point, I just want to know why you keep showing up around dead bodies."

"I'm nowhere near that one," I tell him. "And since it will show up in the reports anyway, I'll let you know that when it was living, that particular body tried to kill me."

"This is the same killer from the train?" Mayfield asks.

"Yes. I'm pretty sure it is," I confirm. "At the very least, he's affiliated with the killer from the train. This man tried to kill me in a hospital in Quantico, as well."

"Then where's the note?" Legends demands, almost like he's daring me to answer him. "You had your little escape room going on the train with all the riddles and clues. How about this one?"

"I don't know. It might not be a note this time. The clue could be something else. I need more information about the location. I know you're near the train station, but what else?" I ask.

"That's classified information we are choosing to withhold from the public at this time as it is part of an ongoing investigation," Legends spews out, giving a canned spiel just like he would at a press conference.

"I am *part* of your ongoing investigation," I say through gritted teeth. "The only solid information you have on a serial killer who has so far wiped out nearly twenty people when you include the bombing is thanks to me."

"The way I see it, those twenty people are dead because of you."

My hand tightens around the phone until I'm afraid it will snap. Sam glances over at me from the driver's seat.

"Emma…." he says, both a warning and an effort to calm me down.

"Screw you, Legends. When you have an arrest warrant for me, let me know. Until then, happy hunting."

I end the call with the sound of Mayfield calling my name in the background. Any twinge of guilt I might feel about abandoning him with his distasteful partner is outweighed by the surge of disgust, sadness, and anger flooding me.

"Emma, you can't stop helping them," Sam says. "We've already cooperated with the investigation."

"I'm under no obligation to help him. It was a professional courtesy. But I'm done with that now. He can try to figure it out on his own. And while he's walking around in circles, I'll actually get it done," I tell him.

We get back to the station, and Sam unloads the box of my father's files into the backseat of my car. He gathers me into his arms, and I rest my head on his chest, closing my eyes and breathing in the scent of him as he presses a kiss to my hair.

"I'd feel better if you stayed here in town so I can be close to you," he says.

"I know. But I can't. Another person is dead, Sam. And this one isn't random. He had a direct connection to both Jonah and Catch Me, which means they are converging. We know what they're capable of separately. I don't want to find out what will happen if they crash into each other."

CHAPTER THIRTY

I'm ready to crash by the time I get back to Quantico, but I can't just go to my house and sleep. Almost on its own volition, my car goes straight to the hospital, and I make the all-too-familiar trek up to Greg's room. I called Dean on the way to fill him in on what was going on. He's already waiting for me when I get out of the elevator. A cup of coffee in one hand and food in the other is a welcome sight.

"Did you get much out of him?" I ask.

"Some," he shrugs. "But it's mostly just scattered bits of information that don't make much sense to me yet. Greg says he was mostly kept isolated. Only saw other people when he was taken out to be involved in events."

"Events?" I ask.

"Apparently, that's how Jonah liked to refer to the… attacks, he had planned," Dean tells me.

I nod as I take a sip of the strong coffee. It is not hospital lounge coffee. This is real, from a coffee shop brew. I am deeply grateful. One day I might have to wean myself off of coffee, but for now, it's my lifeblood. The taste keeps me focused, and the caffeine keeps my body moving, even when sleep is far from my grip. I can think back to when it was merely nightmares that chased away the rest at night. Now I'd welcome the nightmares darkening the door of my eyelids. They would be better than what's keeping me awake.

"How revisionist of him," I comment. "Of course, that's probably how he actually sees it. In his screwed-up mind, all the crimes he commits and destruction he causes are good. I wonder who does his catering."

Greg already looks tired when I get into his room, but when he sees me, he sits up straighter, his eyes opening wider with anticipation.

"Anything?" he asks. "Any new information?"

"No," I say. "But I don't think there's going to be. This is on me."

"It's on us," Dean says. "You're not in this alone."

I smile at him as much as I can manage and put down the box of files.

"Greg, I know we've been grilling you, and it can't possibly be pleasant to have to relive everything, but I have a few more questions I really need to ask you."

"Ask anything you want," he sighs. "I'm slowly feeling better. The memories are there. There's nothing I can do about that. I might as well let them out so they can do something good," he says. "He needs to be stopped. You can't let him get his hands on you."

"I won't," I promise him. "We're not going to let that happen."

"What do you need to know?"

"How much about his past did he tell you? He said that you were one of his honored ones at the beginning, and he gave you some details about his life. You figured out he thinks he's my father and that Dean is his son. You knew about my mother's funeral. You knew about some of the things that he's done. How much of it?"

"I don't know exactly. He likes to tell stories. When there's someone he's willing to tell them to, he will happily regale them with tales of his accomplishments," he says.

"How many was he willing to tell?"

"A few. Some because they believed what he believes, or at least he thought they did, and he was preparing them for more. Others because he knew they would never be able to tell anyone once he was done with them. He wanted their last thoughts to be the knowledge of what he'd already done," Greg says.

"He killed people. Not just in the disasters he orchestrated," I acknowledge.

"'Disposed' of them, was how he would put it. When they used up their value or went against him, he made sure they weren't a problem anymore. But it would be almost impossible to link him to any of the deaths."

"Why?" I ask.

"He didn't use a consistent method or dumping ground. He removed all features that connected him to the victims."

"What kind of features?" Dean asks.

"Did the doctors give you many details about my injuries?" he asks.

It seems like an odd departure from the rest of the conversation, and I glance over at Dean. He gives a subtle nod like he's nudging me forward.

"Not many," I admit. "I know that you were beaten. There was evidence of cuts and a few burns. But they wouldn't go into specifics."

Greg nods. "What about my back? Did they tell you which of those injuries are on my back?"

I shake my head. "No."

"My back was cut and burned. When investigators have looked at bodies they've found, they would have found similar injuries. Not in the same patterns, not always with the same techniques. Some would have chemical burns. Some would look like they were dragged across the road. Some were mangled by machinery. But it all had the same purpose. To remove the mark of Leviathan."

"What mark?" I ask.

"When new recruits first join, they are given tests to prove their strength and loyalty. It starts with a tattoo on the back. Marking you for life. At first, it's a very basic pattern. Only a few lines. And as you progress through the tests, more details are added. It's considered a privilege and reward to earn extra features of the tattoo. The highest members have extremely elaborate tattoos."

"He tattooed you?" I ask.

"Not with my permission," Greg says.

Letting out a breath, I let that idea roll through my head. I'll never know what really happened to him in those two years he spent with Jonah. He'll tell what he has to, but he will probably always keep some details locked inside.

"So, removing the tattoo was a final act of dismissal," I muse. "He doesn't want these people linked to him in any way; he doesn't want anyone being able to uncover Leviathan. But it's also cutting them off, figuratively and literally, from the rest of the organization. It's a tangible act of retribution. For doing something wrong. For disappointing him. For no longer having value. I would assume it usually happens before death?"

"For those who are being punished, yes," he confirms.

"It ensures they experience the full suffering, both physical and emotional, of the entire experience. A hallmark of cult behavior. Being disavowed from the group is a humiliation that many find as brutal and intolerable as the physical attacks."

I'm not really talking to either of them. The words just come out from where my experience and knowledge has them stored. Cold rushes to the tips of my fingers, making me grip the cup of coffee tighter. I glance down at it for a second before meeting Greg's eyes again. "The skin on Martin's back was removed."

He nods. "He was disposed of."

My mind starts spinning, something rising up to the surface. I set the coffee down and move the still-unopened bag of food off my lap so I can get my satchel and take out my computer.

"What is it, Emma?" Greg asks. "I know that look. You figured something out."

"Not yet. But I did remember something. Before you woke up and we were trying to figure out what Martin was talking about on those videos, I had Eric dig into the databases." I click open the file I made with notes about the cases and references Eric found. "There didn't seem to be very much. He searched for Lotan and Leviathan and different variations."

"But he didn't find anything," Greg says with resignation in his voice. "The organization has been going on for a long time. It's never been identified by any of the agencies."

"You're right. We didn't find anything that said Leviathan or any reports that mentioned Lotan. But he did find a cold case that mentioned tattoos on the backs of the victims. The bodies weren't in good condition, but the investigators were able to piece together the images with what was left to figure out what they were. Sea monsters."

"What did they look like?" Greg asks, his voice rising slightly in that way it always did when things started cracking on a case.

"Let's find out."

CHAPTER THIRTY-ONE

It takes more than two hours from the time I call Eric until he gets to the hospital room. I got a few bites into the breakfast Dean had waiting for me, but the anticipation filling my belly makes it hard to push anymore into it. Before he even steps into the room, I hear his footsteps approaching the door

"Did you find the case files?" I round on him the exact instant he walks in.

Eric holds up two thick folders and flashes me a smile.

"Right here." He walks up to the edge of the bed and gives Greg a fist bump. The interaction would make me laugh if I wasn't so on edge I could peel my skin off. "Looking good, man."

"Thanks," Greg says.

"The cold case, Eric," I say.

He hands the files over to me as he rattles off the details of the case

"The bodies were discovered fifteen years ago at a shuttered hotel that was undergoing renovations. Two men, both in their mid-thirties, one white, one black. The medical examiner estimated they were murdered several days before they were discovered."

"At the same time?" I ask.

"That's what they think," Eric nods. "They were found in two different parts of the hotel. The details are pretty gruesome."

"What happened to them?" Greg asks.

Eric looks hesitant.

"I don't think you need to hear all the details," he says.

"I know this man and this organization far better than any of you do. I might be able to give you some insight. But I need to know what happened to them."

Eric nods. I find the crime scene photos as he starts carefully describing what happened.

"The first thing that tipped the construction crew about something being wrong was a grappling hook hanging from the roof of the hotel. They went up to see if somebody might have broken in and found blood. A lot of it. That's when they called the police. Investigators followed a blood trail on the pool deck to the edge of the pool. It hadn't been drained when the hotel was abandoned, so it was too dark to see through the water, but they used a pool net to probe the water. The corpse floated up to the top after it was dislodged from netting tangled at the bottom of the pool."

"Did he drown?" Greg asks.

"No," I say, staring down at the picture of the man dragged up out of the filthy pool water. "He was tortured."

Eric nods.

"His body showed evidence of prolonged physical assault with a sharp instrument. Likely the grappling hook. He used it to puncture and claw him until he bled to death. It wasn't quick."

"What about the other one?" Greg asks.

I take out another crime scene photo of a wooden box.

"Is the other body in this box?" I ask.

"Yes," Eric nods. "After discovering the first body, the team combed the entire hotel. They found this box in the basement."

"There are chains on it," I observe.

"They attach to shackles," Eric says.

Dean gets up and comes to stand beside me so he can look at the photographs with me. The next one shows the box opened. The image of the bloated, waterlogged corpse from the pool was grotesque, but what's inside the box makes Dean cover his mouth and take a step back.

"What the hell is that?" he gasps.

"The second man was shackled inside the box. Hairs and bite marks suggest live rats were put inside with him. He was likely covered in food of some kind. His hands and feet were initially through the holes in the box but slipped inside as the rats ate through him. They were able to get out of the box."

"Good god," Dean mutters.

"I can see why you said the tattoos weren't well preserved," I note.

"To say the least. But there was enough. The one on the guy in the pool was stretched, and some of it had already sloughed off, but the one in the box had most of it intact. He was lying on his back, and the dimensions of the box didn't allow for a lot of movement. Something must have spooked the rats, and they got out before totally consuming him."

"The exterminator," I say.

"Are you giving the killer a nickname?" Eric asks.

"No. He already has one of those. I mean an actual exterminator. That's what scared the rats away. It says right here in the report traces of insecticidal poisons were found on the box and the body. Canisters of industrial-strength foggers were in the basement. The construction crew weren't the first people to go to the hotel after these men were murdered," I say.

"So, an exterminator went into the hotel without noticing the grappling hook and tossed foggers down into a basement where a horde of rats were making this man into their midnight snack," Dean offers. "Hell of a job, guy."

"That's what it looks like. The pool is at the back of the hotel, so it would be easy not to notice it." I flip through the papers more and find the pictures of the tattoos. "Can't say the same for these. There are pictures of the tattoos on the bodies and sketches of what they might look like complete."

I look at Greg, who reaches for the papers. "Let me see them."

He draws in a breath and squares his shoulders when he looks at the paper.

"That's it," he confirms. "I haven't seen all of the different versions, of course, but I recognize details. I can draw the one that was on my back if you think that'll help. But that's definitely one of his tattoos."

"But they're still there," Dean says. "You said Jonah removed the tattoos of the people he disposed of. Why would these men still have them?"

"I don't know," Greg says. "Like I told you, the only person I know of who got out of Leviathan alive other than me is Finn. I don't even know if he's still alive, to be honest. He would be the only person who would still have the tattoo and not be active in the organization. Mine was removed."

"So, maybe Jonah didn't actually have anything to do with these men dying," Eric says. "It could be a coincidence."

I shake my head. "This isn't a coincidence. This wasn't random. This is methodical, carefully planned out torture and murder. These two men were found in completely different areas of the hotel, and the killer took his time. He was confident no one would find him. He didn't choose two random people. These men were chosen specifically and punished. This murder was about revenge. He didn't take their tattoos off because it didn't have anything to do with Leviathan. It was personal. He killed these men because he wanted them dead for a slight against him. Not the group."

"Did they ever find any leads?" Dean asks.

"Not even a hair," Eric says.

I look through the papers again to find the address of the hotel.

"This hotel," I say, pointing at the address. "I know the name."

"It was in Florida," Eric says. "Maybe you saw it?"

I shake my head.

"No. That's not it." The realization explodes in my head, and my eyes snap up to Dean, then to Eric. "Doc Murray. This is the hotel where they found Doc Murray's body."

"The body wrapped in plastic?" Eric asks. I nod.

"There was another person wrapped in plastic?" Greg asks. "Like how they found me?"

"Yes. About a year after you disappeared. He was found murdered, wrapped in plastic with documents and pictures with him. No identification. There hasn't been a positive identification, but the evidence suggests he was a man who was last seen in a cabin in a town called…"

"Feathered Nest," Greg finishes.

Cold slides down my head and over my shoulders like water.

"Greg, what do you know about my mother's death? Why did you have Finn put 'Ron' as your middle name at the funeral home?"

CHAPTER THIRTY-TWO

MARIYA

SEVENTEEN YEARS AGO...

It was always nice when she didn't have to pack more than one suitcase for a trip. The more bags she carried out of the house, the longer she knew she was going to be away from Ian and Emma. That night Mariya was excited as she packed. Like she always did, she'd laid out everything she needed in advance to make sure she wouldn't miss anything. After as much as she traveled, it seemed she should be able to pack without even thinking about it. But she was always careful. When she got ready for a rescue, she wasn't packing like someone going on vacation. She couldn't just choose whatever clothes she wanted or think only about what might look good on any given day. She had to think about who she was going to be when she walked out the door.

Mariya couldn't be herself when she left home. As soon as she left the house, she had to shed who she was and become someone else. That woman was the one who delved deep into the lives of people she would never otherwise know. These were women whose existences would never overlap with hers, whose paths she would never cross except for the brutal fact of them needing her.

That was why she had to become someone else. She couldn't think about Ian or Emma. She couldn't be the loving wife and mother she was at home. That person would never know these women; could never get close enough to deliver them safely from the torment. She adjusted herself to fit into their lives if only for the brief moments it took to get close to them. She couldn't risk having anyone around them know who she was or what she was doing. Of course, the women knew. They were ready for her. At least, most of the time.

It was the people on the fringes of their lives she worried about. The moments leading up to their rescues were among the most treacherous they would ever face. They were more dangerous and more frightening even than being held in the grasps of their abusers. It was like standing at the edge of a cliff with a herd of wild animals bearing down and a mass of spikes at the bottom, with only the hope of a net there to stop the fall. The women had little choice but to jump. But those agonizing, paralyzing seconds at the precipice, with only the faint hope she would be there to catch them, were the worst of their lives.

At any moment, someone could betray them. Someone could shatter the thin shield of protection, and it wouldn't just be the woman's life that was at risk. Mariya learned early to meld into their surroundings as to not call attention to herself. She didn't want anyone noticing her or questioning her place in the woman's life. It wasn't so easy as to just rush in, take her, and rush out. It took time and planning, and she was never willing to abandon a mission once it began.

She was always ready for what she needed to do, but never complacent. She couldn't approach any rescue the way she had the one before or the one before that. Each one was unique, even if it sounded like the same story she heard a thousand times over. She always had to remember that. Each of these women were people. Souls. And the stories weren't always the same. As much as people might want to think it was always a bad husband, or a dangerous boyfriend, those weren't always the case. She carried women and children out of cults, away from parents who held them captive, from people who pretended to be their friends and then enslaved them. Each one had a story, and each one deserved for that story to continue.

It was fulfilling, but it also left her aching. By the time she handed the rescued off to the next link in the chain, she felt drained and ready to be herself again. She needed Ian and Emma. She needed to savor her home and a life where she never had to hide.

That's why she was so excited that night as she finished packing for this mission. It might not be as smooth and easy as the last one, but it would be fast, and then she would be home. Home to be with her family for the next few months. She wasn't stopping. She would never stop as long as she had the ability to help. But she was taking some time for herself and her family. Others on the team would handle things until she came back.

Emma didn't know yet. Mariya was waiting to tell her until Easter morning. She couldn't wait to see her face.

Ian came into the room and watched her as she put the last of her things into her bag. He didn't say anything as he walked with her to the door.

"I won't be long," she promised. "Just a few days."

"I know," her husband said, wrapping his arms around her. "But I always miss you."

"And I always miss you. But it won't be for long this time; then you won't have to miss me for weeks. I'll be around so much you'll get sick of me."

He kissed her.

"I could never get sick of you."

"I'm going to hold you to that. I love you, darling."

"I love you."

"Don't forget to finish Emma's basket. There are two bags of jelly beans in the closet. Remember, she hates the licorice and cinnamon ones, so you'll have to take those out. Put the licorice ones aside for me."

"And cast the cinnamon ones out into the darkness, I know," Ian said.

Mariya smiled and put her bag down.

"I'll be right back."

She ran up the stairs to her daughter's room. Emma was already sleeping; her blond hair spread around her on her pillow, and one arm crooked over her head. She was wearing her favorite nightgown, the one she said made her feel so pretty. Mariya lowered herself to her knees beside the bed and gently brushed her hand along Emma's forehead. She sang to her softly, not wanting to wake her, but hoping the words of the Russian lullaby she'd sung since Emma was born drifted into her dreams and kept her safe until she came back.

Mariya could have stayed there all night just watching her little girl sleep, but she needed to go. She touched a kiss to Emma's forehead and left the room. Just as the door closed behind her, she opened it again, getting one more glimpse.

"Do you really have to leave?" Ian asked, pulling her into his arms.

"Yes, love. You know I do," Mariya said, looping her slim, graceful arms around his neck. "She needs me."

"I know she does," he sighed. "Have I told you recently how incredible you are?"

Mariya grinned and touched her soft mouth to his.

"I won't be gone long. Then, Easter," she said happily.

"Did you kiss Emma good night?" he asked.

"Yes. Of course I did. When she wakes up in the morning, make her pancakes. I left cookie cutters on the counter so you can make them into the shapes of flowers for her. She can help you boil some eggs so they can be in the refrigerator for Sunday."

"Do you think you'll be able to call?" he asked.

"I don't know, darling. I will if I can," she told him.

"Don't, if it's too dangerous. You know we'll be here."

"I know you will. I love you," she said.

"I love you, too," he told her. He brought her close and kissed her.

"I'll see you soon," she whispered.

He walked her out to the car and kissed her one last time through the window.

"Do you have everything you need?" he asked.

"I think so. Goodbye, my love."

She was halfway to the airport when she realized she didn't have her phone. So accustomed to it being in her purse, she'd forgotten it was having problems earlier. Ian had it in his office, trying to repair it. She glanced at the clock on the dash. Her name was on the manifest for a flight at midnight, but the actual plane she was using, a tiny private one she wasn't looking forward to boarding, was an hour later than that. It gave her just barely enough time to go back to the house. Traveling without the phone would be far too dangerous. She couldn't make contact the way she needed to or follow a rescue timeline perfectly timed down to slivers of seconds.

She got back and asked the driver to wait for her and rushed toward the back of the house. She didn't want to disrupt anyone or even have Ian know she came home. He would worry about her too much if he knew she'd made a mistake. She wanted him to be at ease, to relax, and know she would soon be home to him. Rather than going through the front door, she moved around the side of the house and into the backyard. She let herself in the side door and slipped into Ian's office. There was just enough light coming through the window that she didn't need to turn it on. Her phone was still sitting on its charger behind his desk, and she grabbed it, slipping it down in her pocket.

She took only one step more. Her final breath raked her lungs in a sharp gasp in response to movement in the darkness. There was a flash, and then there was nothing.

CHAPTER THIRTY-THREE

NOW

"He never admitted anything directly," Greg says. "When he talked about her death, it was always that the night she died was the worst moment of his life. It was the night his heart and soul were ripped from him."

I try not to gag.

"That's disgusting," Dean rants. "He talks about his heart and soul like they matter after he sent men to kill a woman for not returning his obsession. She thought he was dead, and he still felt the need to scrub her from the planet for the unforgivable sin of not falling into the arms of a monster who obsessed over her, stalked her, raped her, stalked her some more, and tried to kidnap her daughter."

"It doesn't make sense," I say.

"No, it doesn't," he says. "People killing the ones they say they love never does."

"No, Dean, it doesn't make sense that he would have killed her. Or sent people to kill her. He was completely obsessed with her. He believed he had some sort of otherworldly link to her, that they were bound to each other. I've heard of people killing those who don't return their love so no one else could have them, but I don't think that's what happened here. Look at the way he killed these men. He's the only one who could be responsible for these two men's deaths. They were a part of Leviathan, which means he really did own them. They died two years after my mother did. They were running from him for that long, but they never did anything about the tattoos on their backs."

"They were still loyal to him," he realizes.

"Exactly," I nod. "They were dedicated, even in their absolute terror. They ran because they made the most grievous error anyone in his life could. They took away the object of his full and complete devotion, the woman he believed he would one day have a family with, the woman he believed was the mother of his child."

"And he let them run," Greg mutters. "It was part of his torture. He would have been able to find them. There's no way they could avoid his detection for that long. He let them linger so they would have to be afraid."

"Then what happened?" Dean asks.

I don't realize I'm pacing until I stop. My mind ticks through every detail I know about my mother's death, which isn't anywhere near as much as I have ever wanted.

"The most reliable information I have about my mother's death is that she died in the house in Florida. Her cause of death is listed as homicidal violence. There's conflicting information. Her death certificate is from Vermont, even though I know now she died in Florida," I say.

"Your father was already well-respected in the CIA then," Greg points out. "He was known to the Bureau. It would never be openly discussed, of course, but they can make things like that happen. There just had to be a reason."

"The rescues," I say. "That has to have something to do with it. They didn't want anyone being able to trace where she actually was."

"Why?" Dean asks.

I shake my head. "I have no idea." I draw in a breath and let it out slowly. "She was shot. The evidence always suggested there were two assailants. But how did they know she was there?"

"What do you mean?" Greg asks.

"My parents were always extremely careful when we moved from place to place. We never had listed phone numbers, and our mail went to P.O. Boxes. Our location was never publicly known. It's another one of those things I always assumed had to do with my father being in the CIA, but now I realize it was probably more likely about my mother. She had to keep as low a profile as possible, so she didn't get burned as part of the rescue organization. Obviously, Jonah was dogged about tracking her. He didn't just scrape the surface and find out basic things, he managed to locate us and know where we were at a time when both my parents were making great efforts to conceal our location."

"Exactly," Dean nods. "They knew where she was."

"No," I say. "They knew where she wasn't. My mother was traveling that night. That's been part of the investigation into her death from the very beginning. She was supposed to be on a plane, but she was at the house after that plane was supposed to have taken off. If Jonah was so meticulous that he was able to track her down, then he knew she was traveling. He would know she wasn't supposed to be at the house."

I shake my head, starting to pace again. "Those two men stayed devoted to him right until the end. They went to that hotel knowing he was there, knowing how angry he was at them, just because they wouldn't defy him. These aren't men who would betray their leader by killing the one person in the world who meant everything to him."

"But you just said they did kill her," Greg points out.

"They did," I confirm, meeting his eyes. "But not on purpose. Jonah punished these men savagely. If he wanted to just cover up a murder for hire, he could have snuffed them, peeled them like eels to take off their tattoos, and tossed them into the Gulf. But he didn't. He followed them. He hunted them like a predator and then made their deaths long, painful, and horrible. It was retribution for killing her by mistake. He knew my mother wasn't supposed to be in the house that night. That's why he chose it. He didn't send them to kill my mother because she didn't love him. He sent them to kill what stood in her way so she would."

"Your father," Dean says.

I nod. "But they made a mistake. The lights were off when my father went into the office and found her body. Somehow, they got inside the house and were lying in wait for my father. They must have seen movement in the darkness and didn't wait to confirm who it was. They shot her, realized what they did, and ran."

"Maybe that's why your father brought you to Vermont. He was trying to hide from Jonah," Dean suggests.

I shake my head. "No. He thought his brother was dead, remember? He wouldn't have any reason to hide from him."

"Then why was she cremated in one state and a casket buried in her grave in another?"

"Hopefully, when the petition is approved, we'll find out."

Dean gets a call just as we're leaving the hospital. He talks for a few seconds then turns to me with a blend of regret and urgency in his eyes.

"I have to go," he says. "That was one of my contacts. A guy I've been trying to track down for months was just arrested, and I need to go get some information. Shouldn't take more than a few hours."

"That's fine," I tell him. "You go do what you need to do. I'm just going to take a shower and try really hard to get some sleep."

"Are you sure?" he asks. "I can stay with you tonight and go tomorrow if you don't want to be alone."

"I'm sure," I insist. "I'll call Bellamy and see if she can come over. She's gotten pretty used to being my full-time babysitter at this point."

"Hey, not full time," he teases. "I get at least a little bit of credit."

"You don't get any credit," I fire back. "Being a blood relative comes with certain responsibilities."

We smile at each other. We haven't had the chance to really talk about the revelation that we're cousins or what that means for our families. I don't even know how to talk about it. It feels like such a big deal and nothing at the same time. I've grown up without much of a family, so suddenly adding a cousin is strange and exciting. But I don't know if it actually changes anything. Either way, it's not something we've had the time to devote to, but it's fun to give a little bit of a reminder. If nothing else, reminding him that I am his cousin might help to take the edge off the unpleasant reality of Jonah being his father.

"My office isn't far from here, so it really shouldn't take all that long."

"Your office is close to here?" I ask.

He pauses and gives me a hint of a smile.

"Yeah," he says. "When I left the military and had to decide where to settle down and start my business, this was the place that felt right. Turns out there's lots of work in D.C. for a private investigator. Who'd have thought?"

We part ways in the parking lot, and I head home. Bellamy hasn't answered yet, but I leave her a message and stop at an all-night convenience store for some snacks. If sleep continues to elude me tonight, at least my late-night TV binge will be in good company.

I get to my house and do the quick check of the area I've gotten into the habit of doing each time I return home. Everything looks exactly as I left it, but when I unlock the door and step inside, I realize that's not quite the case.

A heart-shaped box of chocolates sits on the coffee table with a note beside it. My skin goes cold until I realize it's after midnight. It's Valentine's Day. The holiday completely slipped my mind, but obviously, Sam had something up his sleeves. I smile, drop everything in my arms down on the chair, and walk over to the table.

"Sam?" I call out as I sit on the couch and take the top off the box to snag my favorite dark chocolate dipped coconut. "I'm home. This is a wonderful surprise."

"Yes, it is."

The voice comes out of the darkness at the back of the house and the back of my mind. It's wrenched from a night so long ago, barely audible from the tiny attic room where Mama sang to me to keep me calm. The chocolate drops from my fingertips as I look up and see glassy eyes and a jagged scar.

"You."

"Hi, Emma."

CHAPTER THIRTY-FOUR

Jonah takes a step toward me, and I stand up.

"Happy Valentine's Day, Emma," he says with a magnanimous grin on his face.

"What are you doing in my house?" I growl.

He cringes slightly.

"What kind of way is that to talk to me? Aren't you happy to see me?" he asks.

"Why would I be happy to see you?" I look down at my hand and see chocolate melted onto my fingertips. "Oh, no."

I grab a handful of tissues out of the box on the end table and spit into them. Scraping my tongue with my teeth, I try to get as much of what part of the candy might linger there out. I only took one bite, but that could be enough.

"What are you doing?" he asks. "Don't you like your treat?" He watches me for a few seconds, then seems to realize what I'm doing. "You don't think they're poisoned, do you? You don't have to worry about anything like that, Emma. I would never hurt you. I just wanted to bring my little girl a Valentine. I've never gotten to do that before."

"I'm not your little girl," I tell him firmly.

He gives me a simpering look like he's just seen a small child try to take a bite out of a wax apple.

"Oh, sweetheart. I know it's hard for you to understand. It's so much for you to have to learn and wrap your head around," he says, coming toward me.

"Stay away from me," I warn him, my hand hovering to my holster.

"Please don't be like this. I've waited so long to tell you the truth."

"You've waited so long to tell me what your deluded mind thinks is the truth. I am not your little girl. You are not my father. You never have been. You are a rapist and a murderer and a terrorist who has lived your life obsessed with your brother's wife," I snap.

He looks almost stung by the comments.

"Did she tell you that?" he asks. "Or did he? He has spent your entire life lying to you and making you believe what he wanted you to."

"All he wanted was to protect me. Ian Griffin is my father. You are nothing but a delusional murderer. You killed my mother," I say.

Any fear I might have felt when I first saw him disappears and cold, angry defiance replaces it.

"No," he says, shaking his head adamantly. "No, I did not."

"It might have been another man's finger that pulled the trigger, but every drop of my mother's blood is your fault. She died because of *you!* Because you sent a man stronger than you to do a job. You might as well have slaughtered her yourself."

"You don't understand, Emma. I didn't hurt your mother. I would have never hurt her. I loved Mariya. I was trying to protect her. Your father was standing in the way. It was always Mariya and me. From the very first moment we saw each other, we had a connection. We were meant to be together. Not her and Ian. He stole her and kept her away from me. Then he stole you. I had to free her. I had to take her away from that life and give her the one she deserved. The both of you deserved," he argues.

"You were going to free us by having your henchmen murder my father? You were going to allow him to be killed while I was in the house. What was supposed to happen to me? How was I supposed to deal with that?" I snap.

"I was waiting. As soon as it was done, I was going to come take you. Then I could tell you the truth. With Ian gone, your mother and I could finally be together, and we would be able to be the family we were supposed to be. You wouldn't have to keep struggling."

"I didn't struggle," I correct him. "My parents never let me struggle. I had a happy childhood right up until the day you destroyed that by hiring men to gun my mother down. Actually, no. Let me correct myself. You didn't *hire* them. That would imply you saw them as people and that you gave them some sort of compensation. You ordered them to do it."

"That's right," he says. "You see, that's what I've been trying to make you understand. I have power, Emma. Control. Wealth. Influence. People revere me."

"They're terrified of you because you're insane and likely to kill them on sight. Those that don't feel that way are just as sick as you are."

"We aren't sick. We just see the world for what it is and what it can be. Everyone is sleeping. Don't you know that? Everybody walks through their lives and thinks they're experiencing everything, but they're asleep. They don't even know what's going on around them," he says.

I hold up a hand.

"Spare me, Jonah. I've heard the spiel. Greg told me about the massive bowl of Froot Loops you call your philosophies. You didn't destroy him. You tried, but he was stronger than you thought. Smarter. More resilient."

"He could have had everything. You can. I want to show you the life you were meant to have. It's your birthright, Emma."

"Stop saying that," I spit at him.

"I won't. It's the truth. And one day, you'll understand that. You'll appreciate everything I've done for you and finally take your place."

"I don't need to understand anything," I tell him. "I am fully aware of what's going on. Tell me, Jonah. How does it feel to have to create a cult just so people will pay attention to you?"

"I did not create Leviathan. Leviathan created me. It has been for far longer than I have. How could I resist it? My parents gave me a name that readied me for it. I waited my entire life for Leviathan. And when I found it, it took me within itself and nurtured me into what I am. I rose to the top. I became Lotan, and there has never been anything like me. I will bring about a world, unlike anything anyone has ever seen. Don't you want to be a part of that, Emma?"

"I don't want to be a part of anything that has to do with you," I say through gritted teeth.

This seems to be what finally snaps him. His face drops, and he reaches into his back pocket. I finally place my hand on my gun.

"Emma, please. I'm unarmed. There's no need for this. After everything I've done for you, I thought you would have more appreciation. I hoped you would feel the connection between us and know you were always meant to be with me. But I can see it's going to take more time than that. Don't worry; I forgive you. I don't blame you. You were abused and misled by an evil, heartless man. You can't help but be confused," he says.

"Don't you dare talk about my father that way," I say. "The only one confused here is you. But maybe a few decades behind bars will make things clearer for you."

In one fast motion, quicker than I can blink, he lunges for me. I draw my gun, but he somehow slides underneath my stance and knocks my arm to the side, sending it skittering out of my grasp. I try to reach for my phone, but he grabs both wrists with an impossibly tight grip and snaps handcuffs on me.

"Don't fight me. Don't make this harder than it has to be. Just come along with me. Everything will be alright. I promise," he says.

"And let you do to me what you did to Greg? What you did to the men who killed my mother?"

I struggle against his grip, trying to kick out at him with my legs, but he applies pressure to my knees and then binds my ankles together with a zip tie.

THE GIRL AND THE DEADLY END

"I told you, Emma, I won't hurt you. I would never hurt you. I've waited your entire life to have you, and I'm not letting you go," he says. "And soon we will bring your brother into our family. You'll like that."

"Dean is not my brother," I say, finally managing to maneuver, so I wrench myself free of his grasp despite being on the floor now. "But you can't stand that truth, either. Because it means you killed another woman for no reason. Did you even bother to find out her name, or did you just call her Mariya?"

"Her name was Natalia," he says. "And I didn't kill her. I wanted nothing to do with her, but she wasn't worth the energy and effort to kill. I even might have had a fondness for her. She would never be anything like your mother, but she made life bearable for a short time after Ian manipulated your mother away from me again."

"You mean after my mother got the morning after pill and cut you out of her life," I say.

Jonah's jaw twitches. He twists his head slightly, stretching his neck back and forth.

"That's enough. It's time to go," he growls.

"That's the first true thing you've said tonight," I respond.

He lunges for me again. I throw my momentum to roll out of his way, moving for the front door, but his position gives him the advantage, and he cuts me off before I can get there. His hand goes to his pocket again, and he pulls out a syringe.

"I didn't want to have to do this, Emma. I didn't want to think you would resist me so much. I hoped you would be a sweet little girl and cooperate with me," he says.

I need him to stop saying my name. It sounds slimy and manipulative, and every time he says it, I want to claw it off my skin.

"I'm not a little girl!"

He glances at the syringe in his hand.

"Do you remember Ian sedating you when you were? He would put you to sleep and keep you that way so he could move you around the country, hiding you from me."

His voice is getting angrier, and I notice his hand shaking just slightly. Tension is winding up inside him like a taut wire, threatening his control. Slowly, without drawing attention to my movements, I reach as well as I can with the handcuffs to the zip ties on my ankles, slowly depressing the tiny switch holding it in place until I feel it give way.

"He wasn't hiding me from you. We moved because my mother saved other women from people like you. I never even knew you existed. They never said your name. They never even told me my father had a brother. You were erased the second they thought you died."

As I say it, I realize he hasn't even mentioned that. Now, he laughs.

"A beautiful ruse if I do say so myself. It convinced everyone."

"Who was he?" I demand. "Who was the body in the car?"

"No one important."

"You don't get to assign value to other human beings."

"And yet, I do. Every day. He was nothing but a pitiful worshipper. If he knew, he wouldn't mind what happened to him. He would have been honored to give up his life for his leader. I did what I had to do to protect myself and ensure I would still have the chance to claim you," he says.

"And more than two decades later, you still haven't," I taunt.

"Something I intend to rectify immediately."

Jonah slashes at me with the syringe. I wrench out of the way enough for him to miss me. I scramble for the front door, but he grabs the back of my shirt and yanks me back away from it. We hit the floor hard, my handcuffed hands around his wrist, struggling to hold the needle away from me. I pull my knee up and bury it in his ribcage. The shock of pain is enough to loosen his grip, and I yank the syringe out of his hand. I press the plunger to release the liquid inside and throw the needle across the room before surging up to get out of his hands.

He grabs me by the ankle and pulls hard enough to yank me down to the ground. I land hard on my handcuffed wrists and cry out as the metal cuts into my skin.

"I'm sorry that happened to you," he says. "I don't want to hurt you. But you have to learn."

He wipes a small amount of blood from his mouth and stares down at me. I glare back, directly into his eyes. Eyes that are the same as my father's.

The same as mine.

"What did you do to Ron Murdock?" I growl.

Jonah makes a sound, almost like a laugh and stoops low, pulling me up to my feet.

"He got what he deserved. He should have protected your mother that night. If he had done his job, it wouldn't have been her in that house."

"You were in Feathered Nest," I say.

"No. I sent a hunter after him. It took years to track him down. It seems he had a few run-ins with the wrong people and wasn't always available for me to find. But something good did come out of his continued existence. He led me right to you. I am ashamed to say I couldn't find you. I tried so hard, and you were always just out of reach. But he led my hunter right to you. When it was safe for him to return to me, he told me, and I was able to find you. I could get close to you again. Suddenly, I had another chance."

He steps up close to me again, and I bend quickly at my waist, then slam upward, swinging my arms, so my elbow cracks into his face. I pull away and break into a run. But he's blocking the front door, so I run for the hallway.

"You're just making this harder," he says. "You're never going to get away from me."

I get to my bedroom and knock the landline off its cradle. The handset hits the floor, but I don't care. All that matters is being able to dial. I've hit the second one when Jonah gets to my room.

"This is Agent Emma Griffin," I shout into the speaker, reciting my address. "I have an intruder who is threatening my life."

"You don't want to do that, Emma," Jonah warns. "That will make things much more difficult."

"His name is Jonah Griffin. He assaulted me and is attempting to abduct me."

His eyes go wild, and he backs out of the room.

"You're going to regret this."

"Stop!" I shout as he heads toward the living room.

Leaving the operator shouting at me through the phone, I run after him. Handcuffs aren't going to stop me from trying everything I can to keep him here. He's already to the door and unlocking it when I get back into the living room. I find my gun on the floor and pick it up, awkwardly lifting it up with both hands bound in the cuffs.

I turn and draw it on him.

Jonah eyes the gun before opening the door.

"Stop," I order him again.

He runs out into the night. I chase after him. Aiming through the darkness, I get off a round before the lights appear in the distance. The grunt of pain tells me my bullet landed, but I don't know where. By the time the police pull up moments later, he's gone.

CHAPTER THIRTY-FIVE

"I had him," I growl. "He was right there, literally in my hands, and I didn't stop him."

I'm wringing my hands together so hard they hurt as I stalk back and forth across the hotel room.

"You did everything you could," Bellamy insists.

"If that was true, he wouldn't have gotten away."

"The police are looking for him," she tells me.

"I don't understand how he got away. He was running away from the house as the police got there."

"They were focused on making sure you were alright," she says. "They heard a gunshot."

"Yeah, that was me. They might want to start checking hospitals to find him because wherever he is, he has a bullet in him."

"Emma," she says.

"I'm pretty sure I got him in the arm. Maybe the shoulder. I didn't want to kill him. There's far too much for him to answer for to go out that easily. But I didn't think he'd be able to get away."

"You really should try to get some sleep. You went through a lot tonight," she tells me.

"And you seriously think I can sleep now?"

"You need to try. You're starting to spiral again, Emma. You can't let that happen."

"I'm not spiraling!"

"Then you're thinking clearly enough to know how important it is for you to get some sleep if you want to be any good in these investigations. I spoke to the detectives. They want you to stay here tonight. I offered for you to come to my place, but they said you would be safer somewhere more neutral and secure. They have an officer posted to keep an eye on your room and make sure no one gets near it."

"I should be out there looking for him. He's getting more dangerous. I just pissed him off royally. Who knows what he's going to do to deal with it," I say.

"The police are looking for him, Emma. You need to stay here, stay safe, and get some sleep. I've already called Sam and Dean. Both of them know what's going on. I'm going to stay here with you for as long as you need me to," she says.

"No," I sigh. "Go on home. You've already been camping out at my house far too much. You should go back to your own place and follow your own advice and get some rest. I'll see you tomorrow," I tell her.

"I don't mind," she insists. "I'm always happy to stay with you."

"I know, B," I tell her, forcing a smile. "And I appreciate it more than I'm ever going to be able to tell you. Which is why I'm telling you now that you need to go on home. I'm not going to be any good tonight. I should be left alone, so I can think."

She finally nods and gives me a tight hug. My wrist, wrapped in gauze by an emergency responder, rubs against her back, and pain shoots through my arm. It only makes my anger more intense.

"If you need anything, call me. I will come here in my nightgown if need be," she promises.

"Why do I think you might do that anyway just to say you did?" I ask.

She smiles and kisses me on the cheek.

"I'll see you tomorrow. Sleep."

She leaves, and I do my best to calm down. I know she's right. I eventually need to rest, but the confrontation with my uncle has put me on edge to the point I feel like I can't even sit down. Much less go to sleep. I keep going over what happened in my head. It almost doesn't feel real. Like I conjured it all in my sleep-deprived imagination. But the pain in my wrist and the throbbing ache of tension and rage at the base of my skull proves it was real.

I finally force myself to sit and pull out all the files I brought with me. Spreading them out across the pristine white comforter of the hotel bed, I dive into them again. There's got to be something here. Something I've missed. Something that will mean more to me now that I've actually come face-to-face with my uncle and heard from his own mouth his depraved views.

Eventually, I must have fallen asleep because I wake with a start. I've toppled over to the side just slightly, so I rest on the stack of pillows, the light in the room still on. Outside the window, I see the very beginning of morning glowing on the horizon. I get up and step into a blistering shower, taking full advantage of the hotel supply of water to stand under it for what seems like hours. I know there's an officer guarding my room, but I still bring clothes with me into the bathroom so I can change right out of the shower rather than walking back out into the main room in only a towel.

A part of me hates myself for doing it. It was already enough at the beginning of all this to realize I felt more comfortable locking the door behind me when I got in the shower. Now I'm hiding even further. The thought of letting him control me with fear makes me sick.

I walk out of the room twenty minutes later with my wet hair tied up and makeup on. The satchel over my shoulder has everything I brought with me to the hotel last night. I have no intention of spending another night here. The officer guarding the room looks at me strangely when I emerge.

"Are you alright?" he asks.

"Yes," I tell him. "But you can go off duty now. I'm leaving."

"I'm not supposed to let you out," he frowns. "Not until I get the okay."

"Am I being held as a person of interest?" I ask.

He looks confused and shakes his head.

"No," he confirms. "But the detectives wanted me to keep you here until they give approval for you to leave."

"She has approval," a voice says from the elevator.

I was so instantly defensive about the officer trying to force me to stay in the room I didn't even hear the doors open.

"This floor is closed," the young man says.

Creagan walks toward us and flashes his badge.

"I'm authorized. I've already talked to the detectives. Agent Griffin is leaving with me."

The officer doesn't argue, and I adjust the strap of my bag over my shoulder as I fall into step beside Creagan to head back to the elevator.

"Thanks," I tell him. "He was going to try to keep me hostage in there."

"Considering the circumstances, that might not be the worst idea in the world," he grumbles.

"What?" I ask incredulously. "You just told him I'm allowed to go."

"You are," he says. "That doesn't mean you aren't in danger. It would be better if somebody has an eye on you all the time. Fortunately, that somebody is going to be me."

"Then I hope you're up for some good old-fashioned pounding the pavement," I tell him. "I'm going to be searching the city for Jonah."

He shakes his head.

"Not today," he says.

"Creagan, I have to do this. He came after me last night and almost got me. I just found out this man arranged for my mother's murder after attempting to kidnap me and essentially making my family's life a living hell. I have to find him."

"I don't disagree with him needing to be found. But you're just going to have to trust the police to do that," he says.

"Why should I do that?"

"Because you have a plane to catch."

"A plane?" I ask, confused. "To where?"

"Florida. The courts approved the petition to exhume your mother's grave. It's scheduled for this afternoon."

CHAPTER THIRTY-SIX

She's not in there. She's not in there. She's not in there. She's not in there. She's not in there.

I repeat it to myself over and over. Trying to soothe the shaking in my chest and calm the sick feeling that roils through my belly as I watch the imposing piece of machinery carve down into the pristine grass growing over the grave marked with my mother's name.

It was a shock to see the gravestone when we first walked out into the cemetery. I knew it was there, obviously. I'd even seen pictures of it. But actually walking across the grass in the hushed silence and walking up to the gleaming white stone made my legs wobble.

Creagan stands to one side of me, with Bellamy and Dean on the other. She holds my hand as we watch the process in silence. There's an ominous heaviness in the air. It seems like none of us have been breathing. Hyper focused senses let me hear every bit of dirt drop down from the bucket of the backhoe into the pile forming beside the grave. I have the fleeting, bizarre thought that those buried around my mother's grave know the plot is a fraud. That the ghosts know the truth.

And yet a part of me wonders if it really is. Ever since that day sitting beside my father on the couch, staring at the urn and not absorbing anything about the memorial service, I've just accepted that my mother's wishes were honored. I never thought to question whether she was actually in that urn. I didn't even question it when I found out about the grave or the funeral held for her. There wasn't a single glimmer of doubt in my mind until this moment. Yet, as I wait for her casket to rise up out of the earth, I wonder if there was a reason for my father to lie to me. Could he have only pretended to cremate her while actually having her buried?

There's no reason I can think of for him to do that. I can't imagine him not being at her service. They loved each other more than any two people in existence. Nothing would keep him up from honoring her and saying a final goodbye if he wasn't going to be able to bring her home the way he did with the urn.

But there have been so many secrets I've recently uncovered. What if this was a secret kept from me too?

I expected the process to take far longer than it did. After only a few minutes, the backhoe moves away from the grave, and another piece of equipment takes its place to actually lift the casket up. It's so simple but looks in surprisingly good condition for being underground for seventeen years. Bellamy leans close.

"Are you alright?" she asks.

I squeeze her hand and nod.

"I'm fine," I whisper. "I'm glad you're here."

I don't say how much I wish Sam was with me. Just thinking about him makes it harder to hold back tears that have been threatening the corners of my eyes since the plane landed. I'll call him when I know what's going on.

"Are you ready?" Creagan asks.

I stare down into the gaping hole in the earth, then glance over at the casket being loaded into the back of a truck.

"There's no other reason for me to be here," I tell him. "Let's get this done."

"The casket will be brought to the medical examiner's office," he explains to me. "I've already spoken to her, and she understands the situation. She's assured me she'll give you as much privacy as she can, but by law, she does have to be present when the casket is opened."

"Even though there's no body?" I ask.

"According to the burial records, Mariya Presnykov Griffin is in there. Until there's proof otherwise, she has to be present."

The casket is already sitting on a table as we are escorted into the coroner's room at the medical examiner's office. It's cold and sterile, with tile floors and steel surfaces.

"Dr. Kelly McCafferty," she introduces herself. "I'm the medical examiner."

"Emma Griffin," I tell her.

"I'm so sorry you have to experience this, Emma," she tells me. "I can't imagine it's easy for you."

"I'm really fine," I tell her. "Her body isn't in there. It's just a casket."

She nods and holds out a mask.

"I suggest wearing this anyway. Just in case. If you've never been around a disinterred casket before, it can get a little intense. The mask will help," she explains.

I accept it without answering and attach the elastic loops over my ears. She hands masks to the others in the room and picks up a crowbar.

"Let me do it," I say.

"Are you sure?" she asks.

I nod. "Whatever's in there, I need to be the one to see it first." Dr. McCafferty continues to look at me incredulously, but I reach for the crowbar. "I'm not afraid of what might be in there. "

She relents and hands me the tool. Creagan gives the medical examiner a look and tilts his head to the side, subtly nudging her over to the corner. When she's away from the table, I shove the metal teeth under the edge of the lid and pry it up. The wood cracks as the nails release. I move down along the casket to lift the lid at each point that was nailed down. Finally, after what seems like hours but was maybe only one minute, all the nails are pried free. I set the crowbar down on the table.

I give myself only an instant to brace, then shove the heels of my hands hard against the bottom edge of the lid. The hard hit lifts the lid out of the way. I stare down into it. Rather than a corpse, the blush pink satin lining cradles a series of four metal lockboxes. I lift one out and set it on another table positioned a few feet away, then take out the other three and line them up.

"Dr. McCafferty," I say, looking at the medical examiner who is eyeing the boxes curiously. "Now that I've proven my suspicions are correct, and there's no body, I'm sure your professional obligation is fulfilled. Thank you for your time."

She gives a single nod, obviously not willing to resist against my crisp tone, and walks out of the room. When she's gone, Bellamy comes up to me.

"What are those?" she asks.

"I don't know," I sigh, exhaling deeply. It felt like I had been holding my breath since the second she handed me the crowbar and didn't let it out until she was gone.

Dean comes up to the table, a confused frown on his face. "Things just keep getting stranger."

Pulling the first box closer to me, I touch the lock on the front. It doesn't seem to be engaged, so I lift the lid. Inside is a stack of manila envelopes. I take out the first and fold the little wings of the age-tarnished brad holding the envelope closed. Tipping it over, I let the documents inside slide out.

"Oh my god," I gasp.

"What is it?" Creagan asks.

I look at Bellamy and then Dean.

"It's Mama's records," I explain. "All the women she rescued. They didn't bury her body here; they buried her history. So, no one can ever know what she did."

"Or track the women she saved," Dean notes.

I pull out envelope after envelope, looking through the pages, whispering names and trying to fathom the sheer enormity of what my mother did. All these names. All these women and children she risked her life to save. So many lives saved. So many given another chance because of her.

"This is incredible," Creagan mutters in amazement.

"Yes, it is," I say under my breath, staring dumbfounded at the record in my hands.

"Look at this one," he says. "The date on it is from the week before she died." He glances down at the closed envelope, flipping it over in his hands. "This must have been the last time she was in Feathered Nest."

His voice softens as he says it. Almost like he's not realizing the words are coming out of his mouth. But they sink deeply into me.

"What did you just say?" I ask.

Creagan looks up at me.

"What?"

"How did you know that?"

"What do you mean?" he asks.

I take the envelope from his hand and look at it carefully.

"It doesn't say Feathered Nest anywhere on here. All it has is the date." My breath becomes shallow, and spots dance in front of my eyes. "You knew."

"Emma, listen to me," Creagan starts.

"You knew," I repeat more loudly, taking an advancing step toward him. "This envelope has nothing on it but the date, but you said it was the last time she was in Feathered Nest. You knew. From the very beginning. Before you ever sent me undercover there, you knew my mother spent time in Feathered Nest. You knew she worked there and that I was born there. You knew all of it."

"Emma, I need you to listen to me. Yes, I knew."

I slam the reports down on the table and stomp toward him.

"You knew my family had links to that town, and you sent me there as bait," I seethe.

"That's not what I was doing. Yes, I knew about the link between your family and Feathered Nest. There's information about it in the sealed investigation files from your mother's death. The rescue organization she worked for has protected status. The mission wasn't available in the publicly accessible files."

"Why didn't you tell me?"

"You were a minor when she died, so you were never given fully unredacted information. When the murders and disappearances started happening around there and it was evident Bureau involvement was needed, I was reminded of your mother being there so frequently. She was there the week before she died. I couldn't pass up that opportunity to create a continuous link."

"So, you just offered me up?" I sputter. "Without giving me all the details I needed to have, you just threw me into it. Knowing I had no idea. Knowing you were lying to me."

"Emma, that's not what I was trying to do. I thought having you there could be a major benefit. I thought I could help to draw out the killer."

"How comforting," I fire back sarcastically.

"I thought it was LaRoche," he continues. "His father was known for being crooked, and some rumors circulated around that he was violent. I thought maybe his son was following in his footsteps. But you did too. You suspected him right from the beginning."

I glare directly into Creagan's eyes.

"But I didn't try to feed anyone to him," I say in a low, threatening tone.

"She was there, Emma. Right before she died. But nobody could figure out why. She hadn't been to the safehouses there in many years. None of them had. But a witness saw her in Feathered Nest for three days the week before she died. She stayed in the same cabin you did. According to people familiar with the town, she and LaRoche Sr. didn't always see eye to eye. There was some friction there. He was even briefly considered a person of interest in her murder."

I see red, but I force myself to stay calm.

"I was told no one was ever considered," I say, biting off each word.

"The information was withheld to protect the integrity of any future investigation," he tells me.

"Until people started dying again, right? Then you just couldn't resist dangling me in front of the man you thought was responsible. I suppose that would be pretty poetic. Father and son police chiefs knock off mother and daughter nearly two decades apart. You couldn't wait for that headline, could you? Did you have your press release prepared?"

"Emma, it's not like that."

"Screw you, Creagan." I snatch up two of the envelopes and look at Dean and Bellamy. "Make sure these are packed back up and brought to the hotel for me."

I head toward the door, and Creagan comes after me.

"Griffin, where are you going?"

"You might not know what my mother was doing, but I know someone who does."

CHAPTER THIRTY-SEVEN

"Looking a little rough, Emma. You should be taking better care of yourself."

I settle into the blue painted metal chair and glare across the table.

"I haven't slept in almost thirty-six hours. I have flown from D.C. to Florida and back to Virginia. I don't need to hear any of your shit, Jake," I answer.

"Lovely to catch up with you, too," Jake says. "Why don't you tell me what you're doing here. You haven't come to visit me once."

"Forgive me if I'm not jumping back into the arms of the man who tried to kill me and dress up my corpse like a doll."

"Fair enough. So, what brings you here today?" he asks, clearly amused.

I set the envelope on the table and slide it over to him. He picks it up and looks at the papers inside. The bemused smile that's been on his face since I walked in the room disappears, and he shoves the envelope back to me.

"Did you know?" I ask.

"Do you mean, did I know your mother stole my mother and sister from me?" he asks. "Yes, I knew."

"She didn't steal them," I say. "She rescued them. She is the one who took them out of a horribly abusive household."

He scoffs.

"Don't you think I know what kind of household it was? I lived there, too. And I was left behind. But that didn't matter. Not to anybody in Feathered Nest. Not to Chief LaRoche Sr. And not to your mother. She came in and listened to every sob story my mother gave, then whisked her away without even a second thought to me."

"Nobody in town knew about your mother," I point out. "Her life was lived in other towns among other people."

"You don't know what you're talking about," he says.

"She worked at Rolling View Hospital as a nurse. You never told me that. You never said she worked at all, much less that she helped people," I tell him.

"I never knew if she helped anybody at all," he says. "She never spoke to me long enough for me to know anything about her. I knew she was a nurse, but I didn't particularly envy the patients who had to deal with her."

"One of those patients was my mother," I say. "For years, apparently. She delivered me when I was born."

Jake lets out a short, mirthless laugh.

"Isn't that so appropriate? She helps your mother bring a child into this world, only for her to come back and pull her away from her child," he says.

"My mother didn't pull your mother from anything. Alice asked for help. She said that she and her daughter were in serious danger, and she couldn't survive in the household any longer. They'd known each other for years but hadn't spoken in a long time before your mother reached out to mine. There isn't a single word in this file about you. My mother would never have left you behind if she knew what was going on."

"You're going to tell me that your mother and mine knew each other, but your mother didn't know I existed?" Jake asks.

"All of Feathered Nest didn't know about your family. Your mother is fairly exceptional at creating her own version of her life to the people around her. The blonde women you killed but didn't... preserve. Were they supposed to be my mother?"

He gives a slow, single nod.

"Is that why you targeted me?" I ask.

The question just falls out. It's what I want to know, but I didn't expect it to come out quite that way. But once it's done, I'm glad I asked it.

Jake looks me up and down slowly. His eyes scour over the skin he can see, and I wonder if he's envisioning me the way he used to know me. As the persona I maintained while undercover in Feathered Nest. I wonder if he can still see the fire dancing around me when he looks at me. I know I see it around him.

"Yes," he admits. "At first. You came to town with a different name and story, but I knew who you were. I didn't find out until several years later what had happened to my mother and sister. But once I found out, I, let's say, took a very strong interest in you and your father. I was interested to know more about a woman who made her living breaking up families and aiding a mother in abandoning her child."

"That's not what she did, and you know it."

"Perhaps," he shrugs. "But it's all a matter of perspective, isn't it? I knew the FBI would be getting involved as the bodies piled up, and our valiant chief of police would never be able to figure it out. I wasn't expecting an undercover investigation. But as soon as you got to town, I knew who you were. I wanted to hate you. But you were different from what I thought you were going to be. I found myself attracted to you. Of course, I couldn't let myself do that. I knew who you really were. What you really were. I wanted to keep you so much."

I stand up and gather the papers.

"Thank you, Jake. I appreciate it," I say.

I turn and start for the door.

"You did a good job with the Sarah Mueller case."

I slowly turn back around to look at him.

"Excuse me?"

He smiles at me. I'm struck by just how normal he looks. There's nothing about his crooked grin or vibrant blue eyes that betray the truth about him. It seems like an odd sentiment, considering how many killers I've come across in my career, but I try not to think about them as people. It's easier to consider them targets and nothing more. But I knew Jake as just a person first, separate from his crimes. Sometimes it's still difficult to reconcile them. His hold on me is gone, but my sympathy is still there. I still look at him and see a broken, wasted person.

"Crime news is very popular around here," Jake grins. "I particularly enjoy hearing about the cases you're working on. You held your own during everything that went on with Sarah. I was proud of you."

"It wasn't a game of tennis, Jake. She tormented me and killed people because she was mad about the very first murder case I investigated. She made my life a living hell, made everyone around me question my sanity, and threatened my career," I snap.

"I know," he nods. "It was fascinating to watch it unfold. I was impressed by how she manipulated your former cases. Though I'll admit, I was a bit offended to have been left out."

Surprised by the comment, I tilt my head to the side and take a step toward him again.

"What do you mean? Your case was in there," I tell him.

"No, it wasn't."

"Yes," I frown, not believing I'm having this conversation. "She lured me to that old house and chased me around for a while and tried to trap me in it."

"That wasn't a house, Emma. That was a hotel. But of all the ways she could have referenced my case, why would she choose that? It doesn't make sense."

It doesn't.

"She knew," I murmur. "How the hell would she know that?"

"Someone out there knows you, Emma."

My eyes lift to Jake's one more time before I walk out of the interview room.

I'm on my phone before I leave the parking lot.

"Did you get a chance to talk to him?" Eric asks.

"Yes. Thank you for setting that up for me."

"I still don't like that you did it, but I'm glad you're done. Did he give you the information you wanted?"

"Not exactly. But he might have given me something else. I need you to set something else up for me. It might be a little more challenging."

"What do you need?"

"To talk with Travis Burke."

CHAPTER THIRTY-EIGHT

There's no way I'm getting on another plane and going to Maine, so I'm thankful when Eric is able to arrange for a video call between the Bureau headquarters and the prison where Travis is serving his sentence. I'm sure it took some creative talking to arrange the call, but at this point, I don't care. Whatever it takes to be face-to-face with him.

He looks old. That's the first thought that goes through my head when the screen blinks, and Travis's face appears. It's only been a few years, yet it looks like he's been worn thin by the years in prison. He doesn't look at me with nearly the amusement Jake did. In fact, I have the distinct impression he's doing the call under a certain degree of duress.

"What do you want?" he demands. "Don't you think you've already done enough to mess up my life?"

"I didn't do anything to you or to your life," I point out. "You're the one who decided it would be a good idea to murder your wife and hide the body. That's on you. I'm just the one who called you on it. But I'm not here to talk about that. I'm actually here to ask for your help."

That brings amusement to his face. He leans back in his chair and crosses one ankle over his knee.

"Oh, really?" he asks. "The great Agent Emma Griffin is asking for the help of a lowly convict. How ever will you maintain your reputation?"

"Right now, I don't care about my reputation, Travis. And I don't even know if I'm going to be an agent anymore after this. But I need your help. I need to know more about Sarah Mueller," I say.

He looks at me strangely.

"Sarah is dead," he says. "Your boyfriend shot her."

Apparently, watching the news is popular in this prison as well. Good to know the memory of me stays strong in the hearts and minds of those I helped put away. I wouldn't want them to go to sleep at night, having forgotten my face.

"I know. But I need to know more about her before that happened. You know what she did," I say.

He shakes his head.

"I don't know anything about it," he replies. He holds up his hands to show his innocence. "That was all on her. I didn't tell her what to do or how to do it. I didn't even know she was planning something like that. She and I had been cooling off, and I had a new girl."

"I don't think you helped her," I tell him. "If nothing else, you simply don't know that much about me. But somebody does. I just learned she knew far more about me than I thought. And figuring out how she knew that could be critical in solving several other cases. So, I need to know about her. Her friends. Family. Anyone who might have had influence over her."

"What's in it for me?"

"Don't push it, Burke. You've got a long sentence left. Tell me first, and then we'll talk."

He sighs. "It wasn't hard to have influence over Sarah. She didn't exactly grow up with the most loving of family lives and got put through the wringer in high school. That's why it was so easy for me to get her to fall in love with me."

"So, if someone were to tell her she could make it so you were released from prison and the two of you could be together again, she would jump on that opportunity," I muse.

"Absolutely."

I nod.

"You know, I came up to Maine a little more than a year ago to follow a tip about a friend of mine who was missing. I couldn't figure it out. I didn't know where he could possibly be going. But all along, it was right here under my nose. Travis, how many men in that prison have tattoos of sea monsters on their back?" I ask.

"A few," he notes. "Some are here for the long haul, but others come for shorter times."

"Let me guess. They're pretty popular. They always have money on their books; visitors come frequently?" I asked.

"Yes," he says. "They are well taken care of."

"Are you particularly close to any of the men with those tattoos?"

"No," he says. "But there is a guy who came to visit one of them pretty often who I struck up a friendship with. Then he and Sarah got pretty close."

I nod, trying not to express any of the emotions I'm feeling. I don't want him to feel like he's doing too much for me like he can start to manipulate me with the information he's offering.

"What can you tell me about him? What did he do for a living?"

"He's a construction engineer," Travis says. "According to the guy he used to visit, he's some sort of genius. He can design and create just about anything."

"What's his name?"

"Before I tell you. What's in it for me?"

I let out a deep sigh. "I'll make some calls."

"You promise?"

"What's his name?"

"It might not be his actual name. He would tell everyone to call him something else. They would announce the names during visitation, but I don't recall what that was."

"What did you call him?"

"Fisher."

"Thank you, Travis. That's all I need from you," I say.

"That's it?" he asks, obviously waiting for some benefit to come from the conversation.

"Yes. Have a nice day."

I end the call and call Eric into the room.

"I need the security footage from the prison. Can you convince them to give you a peek at that?"

"Sure," he says. "Any particular day?"

"Go back to a couple months before Sarah showed up in Sherwood. I just need to see the visitations."

I put a call into Detective Mayfield to check a few things about Martin's murder while Eric works on getting the surveillance footage from the visitation room at the prison. It takes some time, and eventually, I tip-off to sleep, somehow more comfortable in Eric's office than the hotel. He wakes me up to tell me he has the footage.

"What are you looking for?" he asks.

"Someone talking to Sarah more than the usual visitors talk to each other," I say.

I watch the people streaming into the visitation room and quickly pinpoint Sarah. Soon, the inmates come into the room and distribute among the tables where the visitors sit. Her bubbly, bouncing reaction to Travis isn't returned, but she still sits with him and listens to him with rapt attention. His attention wanes, and she starts looking around.

We watch video after video, watching her start drifting away from Travis more often. She sits at a table with a man and listens to him, leaning into him, but occasionally looking over at Travis. It takes a couple of hours, but we finally get to footage of the days leading up to Sarah showing up in Sherwood to masquerade as my neighbor. I can clearly recognize Sarah, but the man is harder to pinpoint. He stays at a back-corner table and keeps his head down. But on one of the last videos, just days before her arrival, Sarah and the man linger after the inmates return to their cells.

I'm watching them stand close together, then walk out of the visitation room together. Just as they step up close enough to the camera for me to finally see his face beneath his hood, my phone alerts in my lap. I pick it up and see a text from Mayfield.

"That train station is currently being renovated, and new structures are being constructed across the street."

A smile twitches at my lips. I set the phone down and look at the surveillance image again, zeroing in closer on the man's face and a dark wave of hair curling down his cheek.

"Caught you."

CHAPTER THIRTY-NINE

"The visitor's list for the prison lists his name as Anson Combs, but according to Travis Burke, he was known as Fisher. We know from information we got from Greg that Fisher is the title of one of Jonah's highest-ranking associates in Leviathan. I can only assume it's the same person. Surveillance footage has him spending a considerable amount of time talking with Sarah Mueller in the months leading up to her coming to Sherwood. If you'll remember, Sarah used details of important previous cases of mine to damage my reputation. At one point, she used technology to operate my phone remotely and lure me to an old farmhouse where I was chased and fell down an elevator shaft. My assumption was this related to Jake and our final confrontation in his house. But after speaking with him, I realized that detail didn't exactly add up," I explain.

"It wasn't a house," Sam tells those gathered in the room with us. "It used to be, but it had been converted into a hotel and then abandoned."

"There was some work being done on it, but the construction had stalled," I continue. "I realized this was not in reference to Jake, but rather to the two men found murdered in the hotel that was undergoing renovation. The same hotel would later be the site of Doc Murray's body being dumped. The way Sarah orchestrated each of her stunts was based on the timing of those cases. She chose that particular order based on Doc Murray's death, which occurred just before I arrived in Feathered Nest to do my undercover assignment.

"The only way she could have known about that was through a trusted member of Leviathan. Those murders were not done as an event of chaos. They were a personal vendetta by Jonah, something he would have only shared with the people closest to him. That means the only way she would have known of that is through Fisher. Through Anson Combs. He has been contracted to work on projects in the Richmond bus station, as well as the train station, where the initial murders on the train occurred. There is surveillance footage of him at the train station. Not getting into any of the trains but showing familiarity with the area."

"So, what's the plan?" Bellamy asks.

"He wants attention, so I'm going to give it to him. All along, he's been playing this game with me. So, what if I lose?" I asked.

"What do you mean?" Greg asks.

"What if I lose the game? Throw it completely. It would mean I'm not going to be playing anymore, but it would also give him the satisfaction of knowing he won. He won't be able to resist either of them. He'll have to come to me. To encounter me directly for the first time. Up until now, he's done everything at a distance or through other people. But this will be his last chance to confront me."

"What do you have in mind?" Dean asks.

"Eric, Sam, and I are going to have a press briefing. We're going to release a statement that I have solved the string of murders previously attributed to the serial killer known as Catch Me. Through personal evidence and his highly telling suicide, we've come to the conclusion that the murderer was Martin Phillips, who used his position as an orderly at the hospital to dangerous advantage. Including my abduction and attempted murder."

"That should do it," he notes.

I nod. "We will end the briefing with a quick comment about how I look forward to taking some time off and managing some family business in Florida. He won't be able to help himself. It'll be just too much for him to resist. Then we go down to Florida, and I go home for the first time in a long time."

"I called Christina Ebbots," Bellamy explains. "She's finally back in town and was able to give me the exact street address of the house. She says Emma is more than welcome to use it."

"It turns out Christina's father Charles Ebbots, aka Grayson, was the head of Spice Enya when he was alive. She found some more of his records. It looks like he was the one who handled planning my mother's memorial service."

"Are you ready to do this?" Eric asks.

"Absolutely," I say. "This ends here."

It takes a couple of days to get everything put into place, but the preparation is well worth it. The press briefing goes off without a hitch, and the almost rabid reaction of the reporters in attendance tells me it won't be long before Anson hears about it. As soon as the announcement has been made, we all head to the airport. The only one to stay behind is Greg. He wants to come along, but the doctors are still concerned about his condition. They're optimistic he'll be able to leave within the next couple of weeks. The agents who've been watching over him are excited to have him back. I have a feeling life is going to look very different for Greg when he steps out of the hospital and returns to the real world.

Getting everything ready for this operation was such a flurry of activity and tension that the sudden calm of it going into action feels strange.

Armed with my gun, the unlock code for the front door, and every bit of adrenaline and caution I can muster, I stop at the steps to the old house before going in. It's just as I remember it. Like the years have slipped away, and the moment I cross the door, I will slip seventeen years into the past.

I let myself in. As soon as I step beyond the front door into the foyer, memories wash over me. The sound of my mother's laughter floods my ears. I can almost catch the smell of her skin.

I walk over to the front door and press my back to it, sliding down to sit on the floor. From that position, I can see sunlight splashing through the glass at the top of the door, glowing in a late-afternoon rainbow on the stairs. I don't look up. I don't want to see the landing and risk catching a glimpse of myself sitting there, perpetually staring down and waiting to see my mother's face.

It's been so long since I've been in the house, I forgot how well isolated it really is. Far away from any neighbors or main roads, it is quiet, but slightly unnerving. Everyone is strategically placed around the grounds and back at the hotel where the files taken from my mother's casket still sit. Now all I have to do is wait.

With nothing better to do, I go into the living room. I'm drawn to the couch. It's not the same one that was there when I was a little girl, but close enough. I sit where Ron Murdock did the night my mother died. He was there to protect me, to watch over me since he couldn't watch over her. I'm thankful for the memories I have of him now. I only wish there were more of them. I wish I knew his smile and the sound of his voice. The smiles in the pictures of him I've seen aren't enough. I want to know who he was when he wasn't on duty.

I don't know how long I've been sitting watching TV when I hear the wail of a siren in the distance. It's short and far enough away to barely be audible, but it grabs my attention. I move to turn the channel and suddenly feel eyes on my back.

"Hoping to catch a replay of your statement, Emma?"

The voice isn't familiar, but I have no doubt who's standing behind me. I turn to face him without hesitation.

Anson is taller and even more imposing than he looks on the surveillance footage. His black hood is pulled up over his head like it was when he walked down the street away from the bus station, but as he takes a step toward me, he pushes it back, revealing his thick hair tied in a ponytail at the back of his neck.

"It really is too bad, you know," he says.

"What is?" I ask. My hand is already on my holster. I won't make the same mistake I did last time.

"You were so close. But you just couldn't figure it out. Just like I thought."

"That's what this is all about, isn't it? Testing me."

He laughs.

"I guess it makes sense you would simplify it so much. The Great Emma Griffin. People treat you like you're the second coming like you have some sort of inhuman ability. But you're nothing. I had to prove that. I had to prove all this worship over you is ridiculous," he says.

"So, that's it? You just wanted to give me a mystery you didn't think I could solve? To what? To prove I'm human?"

"To prove you aren't worth the admiration. You aren't worth the distraction. It didn't start this way. At first, I just wanted to know who you are. I heard your name every day. I listened to the stories, the dreams, the fantasies. You became everything, and I needed to understand it. I needed to know what it was about you that made you so exalted, so precious. But then I realized that wasn't enough."

He reaches into his pocket and pulls out a pair of black gloves, putting them on slowly before drawing a large knife out of a hilt under his sweatshirt. "I needed to rid the world of you, to bring you down so order could be restored."

"Order through chaos?" I ask.

"I can't expect you to understand. You may be his daughter, but you will never be what he once was. What I believe he can be again. He just has to remember. He needs his mind clear so he can see the truth again. And that begins with you being gone."

Anson rushes me with the knife held up by his shoulder. That one position tells me everything about his motivation. A knife held up above the head is meant to slash. One held at the shoulder gains more force, enough to plunge deep and impale.

I'm able to dart out of his way and run around the opposite end of the couch. I raise my gun and fire two quick shots in succession, but he ducks low, advancing on me as the bullets whiz over his back. I train my weapon on him and am about to squeeze the trigger when a voice behind me stops us both in our tracks.

"Stop!"

I immediately leap out to the side and turn, putting my back away from both men.

Anson's fingers twitch and roll, adjusting his grip on the knife. His eyes both darken and go wide.

"Lotan," Anson says.

My gun held firm in my grasp, I aim first at Anson, then at Jonah, then back to Anson, my eyes darting back and forth to make sure neither one makes a sudden move. Anson holds his knife up at an angle midway between both of us. And from where I am, I can't see if Jonah has a weapon. But knowing him, I'm certain he has something up his sleeve.

We're in a standoff.

I suddenly realize both men have gotten inside without incident.

Where are Sam, Eric, and Dean?

CHAPTER FORTY

My heart pounds so hard against my ribs I worry they'll crack and each tremble of blood through my veins makes my hands shake and my stomach churn. I take a slow, measured step back, but Anson's long stride brings him inches away from me in a split second.

"Don't touch her."

Anson turns his head slowly to look at the older man standing just feet away from him. I didn't turn the lights on while I was watching TV. The sun setting outside creates shadows throughout the room. But they're not dark enough for me to hide in. It's just enough to blanket both men in gray that both conceals and accentuates their features and movements. They both seem larger cloaked in the coming evening, but I can no longer see their eyes or the details of their faces. I inch closer to a table lamp, but Anson points his blade directly at me.

"Don't move," he warns. "This is perfect. A moment better than I could have even dreamed of. Look at this, Lotan. Your worshipped and revered Emma is standing right here in front of you because of me. Because I found her, and I brought her here."

"You didn't bring her here," Jonah growls back. "She made the choice to come."

"Only because she thought she solved mysteries I created for her. And she was wrong. She blamed an innocent. Perhaps not fully innocent, but not a killer. Doesn't that mean anything to you? Doesn't that show you who she really is?" Anson asks.

"You have always been so loyal to me. You are so pliable, so trainable. You've always been quick to do my bidding. With you, I have known I would never be questioned because you had none of your own."

Anson's face darkens.

"How could you say that? After everything I've done for you? The systems I've designed and sabotaged. The weapons I've created. You would never have achieved half of what you have if it wasn't for me. But that's exactly why I needed to do this. It was for you, Lotan. I wanted to remind you."

"To remind me? You've lost faith in me?"

"Yes," Anson says. "When I first learned of Leviathan and heard the name Lotan, I had no idea what it was or what to expect. But so quickly, I learned it was my home. My place in this world. I've never felt like other people. I always believed there was more in the world. More to accomplish. A higher calling. And that's what you gave to me. You taught me about the transformative, primordial power of *chaos*. I woke up. I came alive. The world became a place full of opportunity, and I was eager to pursue all of it. To follow you as you pursued it."

"And like I said, you've been a loyal servant. Up until now."

As they're talking, attention totally rapt on each other, I square myself, calculating the exact angle I'll need to fire. I'll only have one shot at this.

"You threw everything away," Anson says, his voice rising shrill as his emotions start to take over. "You stopped caring! Your grasp on the missions you created started to slip!"

I move slowly, closer to the table, and manage to turn on the lamp, giving slightly more light to the room. Anson whips back around to face me, pointing the blade of his knife directly at the soft base of my throat.

"I told you not to move," he growls. "Why won't you listen? Why won't you learn? You are outwitted. Outsmarted."

He spins around again, and I see the men are now closer. They are gradually easing across the room toward each other like a magnetic force is drawing them. "Why were you so wrapped up in her? She became your only focus. You didn't care about anything else anymore, and your power and control were slipping through your fingers. I had to step up. There's nothing I could do. I couldn't watch Leviathan fall. I wanted to bring you back and restore you to your glory. But if I couldn't, I would take your place."

My heart gives another hard pound. I'm very aware of Anson's peripheral vision. I slowly and carefully lift my gun at an angle. I don't know what other weapons might be among us, so I have to be careful as to not spark the violence.

"You've done well," says Jonah.

Anson looks as shocked as I feel.

"I have?" he asks.

"Yes. You did what a true and powerful leader must do. You recognized the failings of those about you. You became willing to take them down to restore the purity of the mission. Yes, I believed Emma was far more than she is. You've proven that to me now. She wasn't able to complete a basic task set in front of her. She lacks the devotion and faith of heart to believe in who she truly is. You could see that about her, while I was blind to it. For that, I owe you a debt of gratitude."

"What will we do with her?" Anson asks, the words coming out cold and flat. Subservient.

"There's no need for her anymore. She outlived her usefulness. I no longer see a place for her among us. If there is a spot beside me in Leviathan, she won't fill it."

I swallow hard, not letting myself get distracted or overwhelmed. All that matters right now is getting through this. My eyes lock on the knife, and my finger rests on the trigger. If I miss by even a fraction of an inch, the knife could cut open my throat. I take a deep breath and look one final time over Anson's shoulder. Eyes so much like mine stare back at me.

And one eye with a glass shard scar.

In a rapid movement, I collapse my left leg behind me, falling to the floor. At the same moment, I fire directly into Anson's wrist. The bullet hits perfectly. Anson lets out a pained scream. The knife falls to the floor in a spray of blood. It clatters just inches away from where I've moved. I use my falling momentum to kick out with my right foot right in his knee. It's not much, but it accomplishes exactly what I wanted: he stumbles to the ground.

Anson lifts his eyes to me, howling in rage, and clamors to tackle me, but it's too late. The massive man is pinned to the floor, his arms behind his back. I quickly scamper up and burrow the muzzle into the base of his neck.

"What do you think of her now?" sneers Jonah. He looks up at me and smiles.

Of course, it isn't Jonah. It's his twin.

My father.

I pull a pair of handcuffs out of my pocket and cuff Anson's hands behind his back. Leaning down close enough so I can put my mouth almost on his ear, I whisper, "I win."

I get to my feet, and my father gathers me in his arms. His face buries in the side of my neck, I fill my hands with his shirt, clutching him close.

"I was worried you didn't realize it was me," he whispers.

I pull my head back, barely shaking away the tears before they spill out.

"Of course I knew it was you. I just can't believe it."

"There's so much I have to tell you," he says, "but for now, we have to deal with this scum. Do you have backup here?"

"Yes," I nod. "They're outside. They're supposed to be watching the perimeter."

"Call them," Dad instructs. "I'll keep an eye on him."

I hand him my gun, take my phone out and dial Dean. The sound of a phone ringing in Anson's pocket makes my hands clammy. He starts to laugh. Dad forces his face down on the floor, pressing the muzzle back to his neck.

"What did you do to him?" he snaps. "Where is he?"

"Tick tock, tick tock, Emma. Time's running out for the son. You better find your precious baby brother," Anson says in a queasy sing-song voice.

"Your brother?" Dad asks.

"Not my brother. My cousin."

"Jonah's son," he realizes. "Dean is here?"

"He is. He's supposed to be outside with Eric and Sam."

Anson keeps laughing, the sound grumbling against the floor.

"We need to find him. I'll secure him here."

Before he can finish, I've taken off toward the door.

"Emma, stop!" he calls after me. "Don't go out there alone."

"I have to," I call out behind me. "I can't let something happen to him."

I dart out into the lush green surroundings, thinking about what he said. It's the same riddle he's used before, but it meant something the last time. Tick tock, tick tock. I search my memories, trying to remember this place enough to understand what he could mean. Time is running out. What did he say?

I keep moving, not wanting to stand in one spot and possibly waste a single second. Tick tock, tick tock.

"Time's running out for the son," I murmur to myself.

I stop. The sun. Not Jonah's son, but the *sun*.

I run to the back of the house as fast as I can. There's a feature I remember back there that I used to love. I would watch it with my mother, spending lazy days stretched out on blankets in the grass, reading books, and eating tiny treats she baked for me.

The sundial is right where I remember it being. And to the side of it is a fountain with constantly pumped water. It usually acts as a birdbath or just a pretty feature to look at when enjoying the beautiful grounds. But right now, it's an instrument of torture.

Dean kneels at the side of the fountain, bent back with his arms secured around the base of the fountain behind him, and his head tilted into the water. It flows down on his face, making him struggle and cough.

I run to him and lift his face out of the water. He gasps deeply, savoring the air, coughing up a fit.

"Are you okay?" I ask.

He coughs so heavily he can't even make words form.

"Deep breath," I tell him.

I lower his head back so that I can work on the knots holding his hands in place. He thrashes and does his best to lift his face out of the water again.

"Knife in my pocket," he sputters.

I grab the hunting blade out and snap it open so I can cut away the ropes. When they fall free, Dean gets to his feet, wiping his face with his hands and gasping for breath.

"Where are the others?" I ask.

"There was a siren. They went to go secure the entrances. Almost as soon as they were gone, Anson attacked me."

"I know," I say. "He's inside right now with my father."

"Emma," Dean whispers. I think I know what he's getting at, but I see the expression on his face, and I turn to look where he is.

Jonah— the real Jonah— stands just a few yards away. There's blood on his hands and a wild look in his eyes. His left arm is clutched to his side, crudely wrapped in a bloodstained bandage.

I wrap my hand tighter around the hilt of the knife and run at him. He's ready for me and catches me with his shoulder in my chest, knocking me to the ground. My chest burns as I try to pull air back in, and I roll to my knees.

Dean jumps in before Jonah can attack, and they grapple. The fight turns vicious, and I scream at Dean to stop as he gets the upper hand, his fist smashing into Jonah's bloodied face, then wailing his injured arm each time Jonah tries to fight back. But he won't stop. I hold the knife poised, waiting for a moment when Dean won't be in danger.

Suddenly, Jonah gains control. They roll to the side, Jonah's wide back facing up toward me. I leap toward him and plunge the knife down right as my father runs out toward us.

Jonah lets out a scream and thrashes as Dean rolls away from him. Jonah stumbles to his feet unsteadily, fingers clawing at the grass as he tries to stand. He nearly makes it out from where Dean and I are, but Dad steps in and swings hard, smashing his fist across Jonah's jaw, causing him to fall back to the ground. He tries to get back up, but he's surrounded on all sides.

Jonah's eyes burn with hatred at the three of us.

"It's over, Jonah. I beat you," I spit. "I beat both of you."

"You little—"

I punch him in the face, and he crumples to the ground, semi-conscious.

"Do you have any more handcuffs?" Dad asks.

I shake my head.

"No, that was my only pair. Sam and Eric aren't here, and Jonah's hands are bloody."

"We'll find them. But we have to take care of him first."

Dad reaches down and yanks Jonah up by his hair. Jonah's eyes open, a trickle of blood streaming from his forehead over one of them as he stares at my father. Suddenly, my gun is out of my Dad's pocket and pointed at the center of Jonah's head, his finger on the trigger.

"Dad, no," I say, the words coming out of me before I can even think them.

"Why not?" he shouts, not taking his eyes or the gun off Jonah. "You know what he's capable of. He's the reason your mother is dead. He has caused countless deaths and destruction. There's no reason for him to be on this Earth."

"No, there's not," I say, my voice level and calm in spite of myself. "But it won't do you any good to kill him now. Make him face justice. Make him stand in a courtroom and listen to everything he's done. Then toss him into maximum security and see how well he does," I plead. "No more secrets. No more sweeping it under the rug. I want the truth to come out. All of it."

Jonah glares at me with a bloodied face.

"I would have shot me," he says.

"I know you would have," I tell him, moving closer and leaning down to bring my face close to his. "But I wasn't raised like that."

EPILOGUE

"We truly believed he was dead," Dad says as we walk slowly through the house, reclaiming moments and memories we left behind. "It didn't seem possible for anyone to survive something like that. And there was a body in the car. And we decided right then to rewrite history. I hadn't wanted anything to do with him in a long time, and I didn't want you growing up knowing about him. I know it was hard on your grandparents, but they agreed. We removed every reminder of him. Every indication we could that he ever existed and went on with our lives."

"Did I ever know him?" I ask.

He shakes his head.

"No. We were estranged for years before you were born. I started noticing his behavior becoming more erratic. He went off to prison for a bit. I talked to him. Tried to get him some help. But something in those years changed him. Even more than before. He started spewing disturbing, dangerous rhetoric. Destruction breeding new life. Chaos making life worth living."

"He'd discovered Leviathan," I note.

"I know that now. I'd figured it was just some prison gang he started running with. Not like this. But it was years before I started figuring that out. And when I thought he was dead, I believed that was the end of it. I just wanted us to be able to move forward. Then Natalia died."

"You always knew Dean was Jonah's, didn't you?" I ask.

"Yes," he nods. "But Natalia didn't want him to know. She never wanted him to know about your mother rescuing her, or how we were trying to help her rebuild her life. She didn't want to scare him or make him feel guilty about anything. For a few years there, she didn't want much to do with us. Your mother worried she was going to go back to her ex, or to the same sort of lifestyle she had. But we kept an eye on her from a distance. Then she was murdered. I remember my first thought being that Jonah must have tired of her and killed her. And it was such a strange thought because by then we assumed he was dead for ten years. I think that was the first glimmer of instinct that something was not right."

"What about after that?"

"I started looking into it more and digging deeper. I couldn't find anything conclusive, but I found enough that suggested Jonah was still alive and had risen to the top of Leviathan. I still didn't know all the details about the organization. I still don't. But I knew enough to understand the danger it represented. I knew he was going to come after you again. I had to protect you, and I had to stop him before he spiraled out of control."

"So, you left me," I say, a turbulent swell of emotions rising up in me. "Without even saying goodbye."

"Emma, please understand, I didn't do it to abandon you. I didn't want to leave you behind. What I had to do was unbelievably dangerous. I couldn't put you in the way of that kind of harm. So I set things up for you to be safe and taken care of while I was gone."

"For more than ten years?"

He sighs. "No, I didn't think it would be anywhere near that long. So much has happened to me. You know as well as I do that going undercover can be treacherous. But carrying the face of a terrorist to try to uncover his actions brings it to a new level. I got on the wrong side of people. I ended up imprisoned and held captive. But I never stopped thinking about you."

"I never stopped thinking about you, either. I always knew you were going to come home," I tell him.

He pulls me into a hug and kisses the top of my head. As we pull apart, my phone alerts me to a message. I look down at it and smile.

"Sam's doing better," I announce. "He's requesting fried chicken and biscuits. Eric says to add coleslaw, but Sam refuses because it's an abomination."

Dad tosses his head back and laughs. "You have your hands full with those two."

"Three," I say. "You can't forget about Dean."

All three men went to the hospital after the police came to take Anson and Jonah. Dad and I spent most of the evening filling out reports and answering questions, and by the time we got to the hospital to check on them, they were all asleep. Sam and Eric both sustained some minor injuries in an ambush but will be fine. The doctors said they were keeping Dean for observation to make sure the water hadn't caused any lung damage he wasn't noticing, but I'm convinced they just kept him so the other two wouldn't feel like he was the favorite.

"What can you tell me about Ron Murdock?" I ask as we step into the living room.

"His name was Elliot," Dad tells me. "He was a very important part of our lives for many years."

I listen as he shares memories of the man behind the title. He explains the organization of the rescue group Spice Enya and the roles each of the Murdock men played in keeping so many innocent people safe.

"Where was he the night Mama died?" I ask. "I know he came here, but why wasn't he with her?"

"He was where he was supposed to be. They didn't travel together. Your mother came back here without letting him know in time to turn around. I blamed him for a long time, and I will never forgive myself for that. He did everything to take care of your mother and keep her safe. Keep all of us safe."

"I hate the idea of him being in an unidentified grave," I say. "Did he have anyone?"

"No. That was one of the preferred qualifications of the men who took those roles. No families. It allowed them to concentrate completely on their responsibilities. They didn't need to go home at night. I have no doubt that each one of them would have laid down their lives for the cause."

"Two of them did," I say. "I'd like to do something for them."

"What did you have in mind?" Dad asks.

"I'm planning on burying all of Mom's files again."

"That's the way it was done for us."

"I think it's what she would want. And I think she would want Elliott and Doc with her."

Dad kisses me on the forehead.

"I think she would love that," he says in a tearful whisper.

I step back from him and offer a wide smile to lift some of the sadness that's settled around us.

"What do you say we go to the water park?" I ask. "I bet they've added a few new slides since we were last there."

Wiping a tear from under his eye, Dad laughs and nods.

"You're on," he smiles.

Two hours later, after shopping for bathing suits, we're at the old park where we used to spend lazy spring days, and I wished for the tourists to never come. I take off my flip-flops and stand on the cement. It's February, so the heat isn't enough to burn my toes, but the oil of the french fries still stings my lips, so I dip my mouth into my sno-cone to cool it.

Tilting my face up to the sky, I close my eyes and feel the sun. When I look over at Dad, he's stretched out on a lounge chair, his wet bathing suit drying as he toasts. Soon, his skin will be golden.

THE GIRL AND THE DEADLY END

A week later, Dad and I walk into the hospital near Quantico together. It's finally time for Greg to be discharged. I'm excited to introduce him to my actual father. Everyone else is back at my house, putting together a welcome home party to surprise him. It's a strange place to be. Our friendship has actually improved by accepting the feelings we thought we had for each other were never real or right. But I'm glad to put it all behind me and just move forward.

We get to the floor, and Amelia looks up at me with a slightly confused smile.

"Did he forget something?" she asks.

"What do you mean?"

"Oh. I just figured Greg must have forgotten something when he left, and you were coming to get it for him."

"He left? I was supposed to be coming to get him," I say. "When did he leave?"

"About two hours ago. He said his ride was waiting for him. I had to bring him out in the wheelchair by policy, but he only had me bring him to the door. Then he walked right out into the parking lot."

I take out my phone and frantically call Greg. It goes to voicemail five times, then stops ringing altogether. Dad and I rush to the Bureau headquarters. I call Sam and the others to see if they've heard from him. No one knows where he is or why he left the hospital without letting any of us know.

The sick feeling has already started in my stomach before we walk out of headquarters.

That night we sit at the half-finished party staring at the television screen, listening to the news reporter's emotionless voice. Watching the edge of the tide wash up on the blue tarp covering Greg's body, where it lies broken and bloodied in the sand.

A new image fills the screen, a security camera shot of Greg walking through the hospital parking lot with a woman.

"If you can identify this woman or have any information, please contact your local law enforcement agency."

The image zooms in slightly closer, focusing on the side of a woman's face and long blond hair. In front of her, Greg walks toward the edge of the parking lot and smiles.

The End

Dear Reader,

7 books...

WOW, we did it. And we did it together!

I hope you enjoyed this season finale of Emma Griffin and it answered all the questions you had so far.

I appreciate your continued support. No worries if this is the first book you read, all the paperbacks are available at Amazon.com and most online retailers.

If you enjoyed this book and series, please leave me a review on Amazon! Your reviews allow me to get the validation to keep writing.

I promise to always do my best to bring you thrilling adventures.

Yours,
A.J. Rivers

P.S. Do you want to see Emma Griffin tackle new mysteries? Stay tuned...

P.S.S. If for some reason you didn't like this book or found typos or other errors, please let me know personally. I do my best to read and respond to every email at aj@riversthrillers.com

STAYING IN TOUCH WITH A.J.

Type the link below in your internet browser now to join my mailing list and get your free copy of Edge Of The Woods.

STAYING IN TOUCH WITH A.J.

https://dl.bookfunnel.com/ze03jzd3e4

MORE EMMA GRIFFIN FBI MYSTERIES

Emma Griffin's FBI Mysteries is the new addictive best-selling series by A.J. Rivers. Make sure to get them all below!

Visit my author page on Amazon to order your missing copies now! Now available in paperback!

ALSO BY A.J. RIVERS

The Girl and the Hunt
The Girl and the Deadly Express
The Girl Next Door
The Girl in the Manor
The Girl That Vanished
The Girl in Cabin 13
Gone Woman

Printed in Great Britain
by Amazon